SCARED IN SCHOOL

ROBERTA SIMPSON BROWN

August House Publishers, Inc.

LITTLE ROCK

Printed in the United States of America
10 9 8 7 6 5 4 3 2 1

LIBRARY OF CONGRESS CATALOGING-IN-PUBLICATION DATA
Brown, Roberta Simpson, 1939-
Scared in school / Roberta Simpson Brown.
p.   cm.
Summary: a collection of contemporary scary stories set in school, including
"Creature Teacher," "Extinguished Educators," and "Student Bodies."
ISBN 0-87483-496-1
1. Schools—Juvenile fiction. 2. Horror tales, American.
3. Children's stories, American. [1. Schools—fiction. 2. Horror stories.
3. Short stories.] I. Title
PZ7.B816923Sf   1997
[Fic]—DC21   97-23602

President and publisher: Ted Parkhurst
Executive editor: Liz Parkhurst
Project editor: Suzi Parker
Assistant editor: Sue Agnelli
Cover design: Alex Cameron

AUGUST HOUSE, INC.   PUBLISHERS   LITTLE ROCK

This book is dedicated to my very special husband Lonnie (who is my toughest critic and best friend) and to our families, especially my sister Fatima. They are my circle of light!

This book is also especially dedicated in loving memory to a dear friend and colleague, Kimberly Arms Phelps, who died December 12, 1996, at age thirty-five. She loved and was loved by her students, friends, and family—especially her young daughter Sarah. When cancer struck, Kim fought bravely and gave us strength to the end. She was frightened by scary stories, yet taught all of us who knew her a lesson in courage we can never forget. Kim, even though you had to go to your life beyond earth, you will always live in the hearts of those of us left behind.

Acknowledgments

I am grateful to all the people who have helped and encouraged me in my writing, especially these:

A special thanks to Liz and Ted Parkhurst and all the August House staff for having faith in my writing.

To my husband Lonnie, who gives me time to write and never complains about helping me edit my stories or helping me with extra work.

To my sister and brother-in-law, Fatima and Ervin Atchley, who helped me through the illness and death of my parents, Tom and Lillian Simpson. I could write knowing Mom and Dad were being cared for.

To my sister-in-law and brother-in-law, Dee and Billy Hurt, who always listen when I need to talk and give me good advice.

To dear friends who accept me and keep my head where it should be: especially Mary Ann Ballard, Brian D. Barker, Pam Eldred, John and Carol Ferguson, Deanna Hansen, Anne Herbert, Dolores Jean Jackson, Joan Kenyon, Drewry and Shirley Meece, Gail Moody, Lee and Joy Pennington, Bonnie Reuling, Suzi Schuhmann, and Joan Todd.

To all the people with whom I work: your dedication, creative ability, caring, and professionalism truly inspires me. At the top of the list is my principal, George "Skip" Clemons, who has unending patience, and our school secretary, Pat Driskell, a beautiful lady who is one of the true wonders of the world! A special thanks to Adele Woods, a colleague and friend whose dedication to her personal physical fitness program gave me the idea for "Hall Walker."

To all who bought my other books, *The Walking Trees and Other Scary Stories* and *Queen of the Cold-Blooded Tales:* you are very important to me. I am always glad to meet you or hear from you. You are my heroes!

Contents

A Grave Opening

It was opening day. The elementary, middle, and high schools on 13th Street stood shrouded in fog like big black boxes with secrets buried inside.

That was what the custodian thought as he unlocked the door of 13th Street Middle School at six A.M. and stepped inside.

I guess that makes me keeper of the secrets, he chuckled to himself.

He kept more than just school secrets. Like those of his kind who had come before and those who would come after, he'd do what he had to do. He thought of the secrets of the stars. What better place to do studies than in the schools? He chuckled again.

He punched in the code that deactivated the security alarm and switched on the light in the front hall. He unlocked the storage closet and removed the mop and pail. He would clean the front hall before his staff came on duty.

Shadows in the hallway were silent and unmoving, like enemies waiting in ambush. In about two hours, unsuspecting students and teachers would enter and pass. A few wouldn't make it through the year. Those who would die or disappear were the ones he thought about.

He had to focus on his routine now, he reminded himself.

The familiar swish of the mop lifted his spirits like it always did. He went on with his work. He was dedicated. He had never yet failed to be ready for an opening.

Dire Alarms

The early morning fog lifted toward the sun and curled into ghostly wisps at the corner of 13th Street and Waiting Place. It had concealed dark clouds lying in wait to the west of the river behind the school. Low thunder rumbled a warning that the sun was not out to stay.

Brian Beecher stood near the city bus stop and watched his brother Albert escort their sister Aileen to the door of 13th Street Elementary School. He saw the little girl hesitate. That was odd because she was usually eager to go inside on the first day. She'd never been scared of school before.

She must be nervous about going in alone, thought Brian. *I should have walked her to class.*

Brian saw Albert lean over and say something to Aileen. He saw her shake her long blonde hair, pull the door open, and dart inside.

She didn't want Albert to go with her either, Brian said to himself.

He was proud of his sister's attempt to be independent, but something about her hesitation at the school door made him uneasy. When Aileen failed to plunge into something, it usually meant there was something bad about it.

What could be bad here? he wondered.

The school seemed fine to him, but his mom had expressed doubts this morning.

"I wish I didn't have to work, Brian," she said. "I feel like I should take Aileen to school today. I've always gone with her before. At least Albert will be next door at the middle school and your classes at the high school will be close by."

Brian noticed worry lines on his mother's face for the first time. "We'll be all right," he tried to reassure her.

The elementary and middle school stood side by side, with a riveting view from the back windows of the rushing river and the still woods beyond. Right across the street, the high school towered three stories above the scene. There was nothing frightening about the setting. Of course, the 13th Street name could be a little spooky if you were the superstitious sort.

Except for his sister's odd behavior, there was nothing to indicate to Brian that this would be anything but a normal day. That was about to change.

The Chill-dren

Kirk Radborne glanced anxiously at the overcast sky as he stood waiting on the corner of Ashford and Belleview for the school bus to take him to 13th Street Middle School. It was the first day of school, and this was the first stop on the long bus route.

As a rule, Kirk didn't like being picked up first. He'd always go to the back of the bus and sit quietly until the driver stopped seven blocks away to pick up Kirk's best pal, Russell Newman. When Russell boarded, Kirk would yell a greeting, his buddy would join him and chatter about whatever had happened at home that morning, and the silence was broken for the rest of the ride.

But Kirk really wanted the bus to come this morning. The sky was growing more threatening by the moment, and Kirk knew the thin jacket he was wearing would not keep the rain off his frail body.

"Wear your raincoat," his mother had instructed.

"Raincoats are for girls," he told her. "Besides the sun is coming out."

She had gone upstairs to get ready for work without really hearing him. He had grabbed his light cotton jacket and hurried out the door as soon as she was out of sight.

The sun had not stayed out. Now he'd be soaked and cold all day and he'd be in trouble with his mom when he got home. He'd missed several days of school last spring because of colds and allergies, and he'd had to study hard to make up his work. He'd probably miss more if he got wet and chilled today, and he didn't want to try to catch up on missed work again. If the bus would come, he'd be saved.

The wind lashed out at him now and the black clouds began to spit out the first drops of rain. Kirk pulled his jacket tight around himself, but the water penetrated to his skin anyway. He was thinking of looking for shelter when he saw headlights turn the corner.

"About time," Kirk muttered, turning to pick up the bookbag that he had leaned against a corner mailbox.

He turned back, ready to step from the curb to the bus, when he saw a large black car instead of the yellow bus he'd expected. The driver pulled up and rolled down the window on the passenger side.

"Want a lift to school, son?" called the man behind the wheel. He smiled, and Kirk thought the man had the whitest teeth he'd ever seen.

The offer took Kirk by surprise. For a second, he was tempted to accept, for the rain was peppering down harder now, stinging his face. Then he remembered his mother had made him promise never to ride with strangers.

Kirk stepped back on the sidewalk as far away from the car as he could get without stepping on the grass.

"No, thank you," he said firmly. "I'm riding the bus with my friend Russell. Besides, my mother told me I should never ride with anyone I don't know."

"She's right," said the man. "You can't be too careful these days. I should have introduced myself. I thought maybe we met at school orientation last week. I'm Phil Yates, the new counselor at 13th Street Middle School."

"Hi," said Kirk. "That's the school I go to, but we didn't go to orientation last week. Mom had to work."

"I see," said the man. "What's your name?"

"Kirk Radborne," Kirk answered.

"Well, Kirk, you're welcome to ride if you want to, but I won't insist," said Mr. Yates. "I hate to see you standing there getting soaked in this rain, though."

Kirk took a step forward, then had second thoughts. The man was still bending down smiling at Kirk, but Kirk didn't like the smile much. Only the mouth was smiling. The eyes were cold and penetrating like the rain.

The decision was made for Kirk. Headlights came around the corner again and Kirk saw the bus.

"Here's my bus now," he said.

The man in the large black car nodded and pulled

quickly away.

The bus door opened and Kirk hurried up the steps, trembling with relief.

Clouds' Shrouds

The clouds came between the sun and Albert Beecher as he left his sister at the elementary school and hurried toward the middle school next door. Brian stood watching, thinking it was unlike his brother to hurry to school. He could easily see the name of the school—13TH STREET MIDDLE SCHOOL—on a sign above the entrance. The bold black letters against the blood-red background proudly displayed the colors of the school mascot, the Red Demons. Underneath, a cheerful yellow sign—SAFE PLACE—tempered the harshness of the other colors.

On Friday when Brian's mom had brought them to register, she had been happy to see that the 13th Street schools were part of the Safe Place program. It was a relief to know that help was always available here to kids in danger or trouble. Brian remembered how she'd pointed out the sign to Albert, Aileen, and him. He knew seeing the sign made his mother feel better.

Brian saw Albert glance back over his shoulder and then increase his pace like someone trying to get away from something unpleasant. Then Brian felt the first sprinkles of rain.

That's it—it's the rain, Brian thought when he saw Albert hurrying. *He doesn't want to get wet.*

Brian smiled and threw up his hand. Albert grinned and

waved back at Brian. Albert had grown lanky like his father, but he was comfortable with his height and carried himself gracefully like Brian.

Brian knew he should be going to his own classes, but he couldn't make himself cross the street to the high school just yet. He could still hear his mother's voice before she left for work this morning.

"Be sure they're safe inside before you leave them," she had said, almost pleading.

Brian didn't always do what his mother asked, but he'd tried to do better since his dad had walked out on them. He knew it was hard on her with the new job and all.

Brian saw that Albert had reached the front door now. Thunder boomed and a bright flash of light filled the woods across the river. The light by the entrance flickered as Albert pulled open the door, and Brian saw two letters added to the yellow sign. UNSAFE PLACE, it now distinctly said. Brian blinked and looked again. The sign was back to normal.

That flash of light must have been aliens landing in the woods, he thought. Just as quickly he realized he had been watching the sci-fi channel a bit too much. Either that, or he was losing his mind.

Albert vanished through the door as the rain fell harder, but Brian stood focused on the sign. He half expected it to change again, but it didn't. It was just a trick of the light.

Scared in School

But what if it wasn't? a little voice asked in his head.

He fought a sudden urge to run from one school to the other and drag his sister and brother from their classes.

I'm freaking out! I'm seeing things, hearing voices in my head, and getting soaked in a storm. I don't have sense enough to get in out of the rain. Even my little brother did that!

The clouds opened and poured streams of raindrops while Brian dashed madly across the street. When he entered with his hair plastered to his head and his clothes dripping little puddles, he knew he was giving new meaning to the image of a silly sophomore.

As he removed his jacket and shook it, he looked out the door. The clouds were boiling so low that they seemed to have swallowed the schools.

Crybaby, Die Maybe

The bus driver nodded to Kirk Radborne, and Kirk nodded back. He hadn't seen this man before. He'd wondered who would replace last year's driver. Kirk had liked the man, but he'd seen on the news that he had been admitted to some private hospital upstate. "Why did he have to go to the hospital?" he'd asked his mother.

"His brother found him at home babbling about invisible beings who whispered to him, so he had him taken away," she'd answered.

When Kirk discussed it with Russell, his friend had been quick to take credit on behalf of all the bus riders for driving the man insane.

Kirk didn't think the new driver would be bothered by unseen things or unruly kids. His eyes sparkled with clearness and darted with alertness. The driver's expression was blank as he eased the bus forward in the rain. Kirk glanced back as he headed down the aisle for his usual seat in the rear. He could see the muscles ripple along the driver's arm as he shifted gears.

I guess there won't be many fights on the bus this year with this guy driving, thought Kirk.

Neither the boy nor the driver spoke during the seven-

Scared in School

block drive to Russell's stop. Kirk was thinking about his encounter with the new counselor and he figured the driver was thinking about his route.

Russell was standing under the city bus shelter as the school bus came in sight, and he ran through the downpour to board. His red hair dripped and his freckled face broke into a grin as he looked at the driver. The driver only nodded to Russell as he had to Kirk.

"The charm of a rattlesnake," whispered Russell, nodding toward the driver.

"Yeah," said Kirk, "like our new counselor."

"We have a new counselor?" asked Russell. "How do you know?"

"He stopped and offered me a ride just before the bus came," explained Kirk. "The guy gave me the creeps. There was an odd look in his eyes."

"You're beginning to sound like Karen Frazier," teased Russell, pointing to the tall, skinny girl standing on the corner where the bus was pulling up. "She thinks there's something odd about everybody. She believes aliens have landed and are living here just like regular people."

"Yeah," grinned Kirk. "I guess you're right. Mom says her grandmother tells her those wild stories."

Russell nodded.

The two boys watched Karen step into the aisle and stop.

She made a big deal about where to sit every day. Before she decided, the bus lurched forward and she grabbed the back of a seat to keep from falling. Her bookbag flew from her hand and broke open on impact. Something slid from the bag and stopped by Russell's feet.

"Hey! Watch it, Mister!" Karen called over her shoulder to the driver as she struggled to regain her balance. She didn't see Russell bend over and pick up her diary.

He looked at the pink cover with Karen's name in bold black letters.

"Well, well!" he said, holding it up. "What do we have here?"

Karen saw what he had and struggled toward him as the driver braked at a stop where several students were waiting.

"Give me that!" she demanded.

Russell opened it up instead and began to read aloud from the last entry.

"At orientation last week, the new counselor—"

Karen lunged forward and snatched the diary from his hands. Kirk saw that tears were running down her face, but she said nothing. He felt sorry for her. Her mom had died last year and her dad had never been around.

By the time Karen picked up her bookbag, one of the students from the last stop was sitting in the seat she always picked. She sat in front of Russell and Kirk, and took out her pen and

Scared in School

diary. Kirk could see her hand shake as she wrote.

Russell leaned forward and peered over her shoulder, trying to see what she was writing. She glared at him and covered the page with her hand. When she finished and put the diary away, Kirk thought she still looked sad.

It must be awful not to have anyone to talk to, he thought.

He started to talk to her about the new counselor, but when he leaned closer to speak, he saw tears running down her cheeks again.

It's not a good time to talk now, he told himself. Later, he wondered if it would have made a difference if he had.

School Spirit

There was no logical reason for the needling fear that accompanied Brian Beecher to his homeroom. Albert and Aileen were safe inside their schools and he didn't have to worry about them.

I shouldn't have to worry about them anyway, he said to himself. *That's what parents are for.*

He remembered how it had been before his dad walked out on them. They had moved a lot because his dad had gone from job to job, but his mom had not had to work. She was free to take them to school and deal with their problems. Now Brian and his mother were sharing the duties his father had discarded. He could taste the bitterness in his throat. His dad had promised him a car when he was sixteen. He hadn't even been around to give him bus fare.

He should be glad his mom had landed a permanent job so they could finally put down roots, but he only wanted things to be like they had been.

His mother had tried to make things normal. She had taken Albert, Aileen, and him to their schools Friday afternoon to register and find their classes. The place should look familiar after Friday's tour, but Brian felt lost and alienated. Small groups of students gathered by lockers. Couples walked by Brian with eyes only for each other. He stared at the off-white walls and the cold gray tile floor. He was glad when homeroom was over and he could start first period, even if it was math.

As he sat in math class, barely aware of Mrs. Willis's droning, he wondered what was making him so jumpy. Too much responsibility at home? Too many new adjustments?

No answer seemed satisfying. His home problems were part of his uneasiness, but there was something more.

Maybe I'm just spooked, he thought, *because all three schools are at the corner of 13th Street and Waiting Place.* He was surprised that only a part of himself chuckled at that suggestion.

He remembered that Aileen had asked that morning, "Why would anyone name a street Waiting Place?"

"People wait for buses here," Albert had answered.

Nobody had been waiting there this morning when the bus had let them off. Brian had waited alone while he watched his brother and sister go to their schools. It was there on that corner that he felt the fear for the first time. Even now in class with all the other students around him, he was still afraid.

The bell ending class brought Brian to his feet with the other students. A glance at his schedule told him there was a pep rally in the gym second period. He'd never been in a school before where they'd had a football game so near the opening of school, but this was a small town with a long-standing rivalry with the next town. He'd hoped to make the team, but it had already been picked before he had moved to town. The 13th Street Wolverines were playing the Southern Sabers tonight in a home game. Brian had heard the principal bragging to his mother Friday that the sports program brought the community together and kept the young people out of trouble. Brian crowded toward the gym with the others to get the school spirit.

I'll get it before it gets me! he thought. His amusement at his pun gave way to a chilling memory.

Just then, a shove sent him colliding with the school custodian.

"Excuse me," said Brian.

The custodian leaned against his mop. He nodded slowly, a faint smile flickering on his lips. He straightened and swished his mop along the floor outside the locker room.

Brian looked down and saw animal tracks. What could have gotten into the building over the weekend? They looked like the wolf tracks Brian had once seen while out hunting with his uncle. *There are no wolves here. It must have been a really large dog,* Brian thought.

The cheering inside the gym started, directing Brian's mind momentarily to less morbid things:

Wolverines! Wolverines!
We can beat the Saber's team!

Scared in School

Brian looked at the floor again. The tracks were disappearing with each swish of the mop. Bolting toward the gym, Brian ran inside and closed the door. He sat among the cheering students, his heart pounding.

Opening Daze

When Kirk reported with Russell and the other students to the auditorium at school, Phil Yates stood near the door handing out schedules.

"Hello, again," he said to Kirk. "I'm glad you made it safely."

Kirk felt a little foolish now that he knew Phil Yates really was the new counselor. Yet there was something about the man that still bothered him. The odd look was still in his eyes, but he knew it wouldn't be wise to mention it to Russell again.

Kirk didn't look at his schedule until Russell came over to compare his.

"We've got the same homeroom!" said Russell. "We'll have all our classes together. I heard geeky Karen say she's in homeroom 7A. We won't have to see her except in first period P.E."

When Russell mentioned Karen, Kirk spotted her outside the auditorium talking to Mr. Yates. Even though he didn't personally like the man, he was glad Karen had found an adult to talk to. She looked as if she was crying again.

Creature Teacher

The bright August day six years ago had not been the kind of day that made ten-year-old Brian Beecher think of supernatural happenings. He reserved those things for Halloween, and even then he didn't take them seriously. He didn't know that some day he would. On this particular summer day, Brian was only thinking that it was not natural to start school so early in August.

"Country roads get impassable in winter," his dad had told him. "They start school early so they won't have so many snow days to make up at the end of the term."

So Brian had enrolled in Miss Eliza Green's fifth grade class in a little southern town called Greenville.

At first, it seemed odd to Brian that he should remember that incident in Miss Eliza's class while attending a high school pep rally. But the more he thought about it, the more he knew there was a connection between that bizarre experience and what he had just seen in the hall.

Of course, his dad had been with them then. He was hired at a construction site in Greenville just before school started. Brian had been stuck at home for days helping his mom unpack and babysitting his brother and sister. The one good thing about school starting was the opportunity to make some friends his own age. And to his relief, he had quickly made two new friends, Larry Miller and Charles Cornell, who were also in Miss Eliza's class. They wasted no time in sharing her nickname with Brian.

"They call her the Creature Teacher," Charles said. His brown eyes were wide and serious.

"She's a witch," Larry added.

"There's no such thing as a witch," Brian replied.

"Look at her wrinkles and her pointed nose," Larry argued.

"She has a black cat, too," Charles joined in.

"That doesn't make her a witch," argued Brian. "Lots of grandmothers could fit that description!"

"I warn you," said Larry. "She has strange powers!"

"Don't cross her," added Charles. "Or if you do, don't let her catch you!"

Charles snickered when he said it, but Larry remained serious.

"Creature Teacher!" laughed Brian.

"I wouldn't laugh," said Larry, adjusting his glasses as he leaned closer to Brian. "She can cause bad things to happen to people she doesn't like. Last year, the principal gave her extra duty in the cafeteria, and he had a flat tire every day that week."

"Why do you think that was connected to her?" asked

Brian.

"Some kids heard her muttering something as she walked by the car," said Larry.

"Maybe the kids did something to the tires after she left," suggested Brian.

"Not a chance," said Charles. "When the lunchroom lady yelled at Miss Eliza because her students didn't clean off the tables, Miss Eliza said something under her breath and a dozen rats showed up in the kitchen the next morning! It nearly scared that lunchroom lady to death. She had a spell with her heart and they had to take her to the doctor."

"That was the only kind of spell in the whole thing," scoffed Brian. "I think you guys tell this tale to all the new students."

"You'll see," said Larry.

Brian did see! Five years had passed, but he could still picture it as clearly as the day it had happened.

He relived in his mind that day in the fifth grade when they'd had the food fight in the cafeteria. Some students had brought their own lunches, but others were enjoying the pizza special. Brian was sitting at a table with Charles and Larry watching Larry try unsuccessfully to get Gena Bolling's attention. A chortle from Charles made Larry determined to succeed.

Larry glanced around to make sure no adults were watching, carefully picked up a large thick slice piece of pizza saturated with thin, runny sauce and flipped it on Gena's white blouse. Startled, Gena watched it stick and then slide down, leaving a nasty red blotch of sauce. She glared at Larry as she stood up and dumped the contents of her chocolate milk carton on Larry's head. Laughter erupted all around the table. Seeing the brown liquid run down Larry's face and neck inspired the other students to see what they could add to the funniest sight they had seen all year. They filled the air with flying buns, bologna, and the rest of the pizza until Miss Eliza's voice cut through it all.

"Stop it this instant!"

Everyone stopped, but a large leaf of lettuce, already airborne, plopped on the floor next to her.

"You will clean up this mess at once," Miss Eliza ordered in her coldest voice. "Each of you will bring your lunch and eat silently in my room for a week. And you, Larry Miller, will come with me to the principal's office right now since you started it."

How had she known that? Larry had made sure she was out of the cafeteria before he threw the pizza.

That had been on a Friday. Larry had been suspended for three days. As the class ate lunch silently in the classroom with Miss Eliza, they pictured Larry eating and watching TV at home. Three long, hot days passed.

When Larry came back on Thursday, he looked pale and thin. During break before the last class, he called Brian and

Charles over to his locker.

"Miss Eliza put a spell on me," he announced. "I was sick the whole time I was off. I couldn't keep a thing down."

"Because of the food fight?" asked Charles.

"I think so," said Larry, "and she's not going to get away with it. I've got a little surprise for her in this bag that'll make her puke her guts out!"

Brian and Charles moved closer. Larry opened the bag and held it out.

"Look!" he grinned.

They looked and turned their heads, gagging in unison.

"What's that awful smell?" asked Charles.

"Dead frogs!" Larry told them. "Dead rotten frogs for the old witch! I killed them myself and put them out in the sun to rot. You know how hot it's been. They've had Friday night, Saturday, Sunday, Monday, Tuesday, and Wednesday to get good and ripe!"

"You're not really going to hand her that bag, are you?" asked Brian.

"Just watch me!" said Larry.

"But she'll do something really awful to you," said Charles.

"Nothing could be worse than what she did last week," said Larry.

The boys were startled by the swish of a mop behind

them. They whirled and saw the custodian near the lockers. Larry closed the bag just as the tardy bell sounded, and the three boys hurried to the classroom door.

"Do you think he heard us?" whispered Charles as they walked to their seats.

"No," said Larry. "He would have taken the bag if he'd heard me. He and Miss Eliza are friends."

"I don't know," said Brian. "Maybe you'd better forget about getting even and throw the bag in the trash. You've already been suspended for three days. Do you want to get in trouble again?"

"It would be worth it!" said Larry.

"Sit down and be quiet, boys," Miss Eliza ordered.

The boys took their seats quietly. Larry put the bag on the floor beside his desk.

"What's in the bag, Larry?" asked Miss Eliza.

Larry glanced at Brian and Charles, and then looked at Miss Eliza. He knew what was coming next.

"Bring me the bag, Larry," she demanded.

For once, Larry was quick to obey. He took the bag and held it out to her, but she didn't reach for it as he thought she would. What she did was totally unexpected. Miss Eliza began to laugh, a low cackling laugh that grew louder and louder!

She looked at the class, but nobody moved. They sat staring as if they were under a spell. Then Miss Eliza pointed her finger at the bag Larry was now clutching. At once, the bag began to bulge and wiggle. It jumped from Larry's hand and flew open on the floor. Frogs of all sizes came spilling out, tumbling over each other, hopping in all directions. They had somehow come to life, even though they still smelled dead and rotten!

The stench woke the class from under its spell. They dropped books and turned over desks in a mad dash for the hall, with those hideous living-dead frogs croaking at their heels.

Miss Eliza's laughter faded as Brian fled with the others. Brian didn't stop running until he got home.

Brian had never had to go back to that school. His father had been fired that day, and he announced they would be moving that weekend to another town. Brian eagerly volunteered to stay home on Friday and help get ready to move. His father had agreed, and Brian was happy for once to be moving on.

Charles had called Brian to say Larry was suspended again and that he and Brian might have to go to the principal on Monday to tell what they knew about the frogs. Brian hoped not. He couldn't imagine what he would say. He'd have to tell the principal that he saw dead frogs come alive. And he hardly wanted to do that! He'd look like a total crazy geek talking about dead frogs hopping back from the dead.

But on Monday, Brian was far away and the episode in Miss Eliza Green's class was fading from his mind. He had kept it out until this morning. He realized how frightened he had been

Scared in School

because of something he couldn't logically explain. He thought of Aileen and wondered if a similar scary memory had made her hesitate at the school door that morning. Again, he had the strange feeling that he should hurry to her room to get her from class, but he told himself that was silly. When he thought back later, he knew he would have gone to her regardless of the consequences if he had known then about the events that would be set off by the 13th Street Elementary School's seating chart.

Death Row

Aileen Beecher slipped into her classroom and sat in the last seat in the first row, as far from the window as she could get. She didn't want to show how frightened she was of the storm. Now that it had almost passed over, she couldn't understand why she was still scared. She had to force herself to listen to the teacher.

"I've made a seating chart until I get to know you," said Mr. Decker. "Move quickly to your seats when I call your name."

The 13th Street fifth-grade class groaned in unison.

"Come on," he coaxed. "It won't be for long."

A few groans followed, but not as many as before.

"We'll start with row one," he said. "Annette Adalard, Alan Bailey, Aileen Beecher, Brett Burgess, Candace Golding, and Harrison Monroe."

Mr. Decker looked up to see that every one was in the correct seats. Harrison was the only one standing.

"Harrison Monroe," said Mr. Decker, "take the last seat in the first row, please."

"I'd rather not, sir," said Harrison, "if you don't mind."

"Why not?" asked Mr. Decker. "Can't you see the board?"

"No, that's not it," said Harrison.

Scared in School

"Then what's the problem?" asked Mr. Decker.

Those who had attended school with Harrison before were listening intently now for his answer. He was the class clown and they were all wondering what he was up to.

"It's cursed, sir," Harrison said, very seriously.

"Cursed?" asked Mr. Decker.

"Yes, sir," Harrison answered. "That used to be Henry Huxley's seat. He got hit and killed by a car last year. He told everybody before he died that he'd come back and always sit in that seat. He said anybody else that sat in it would die."

Several of Harrison's friends had to choke back giggles, but they all managed to keep their faces serious and nod in agreement.

Mr. Decker remembered that someone had mentioned a death to him when he'd been in his room putting up a bulletin board the first day he came to the school. A boy *had* been struck by a car and killed in front of the school last year, but he couldn't recall the details. The name might have been Henry Huxley, but he didn't know what room the boy had been in last year. He'd have to ask someone about it later. He had Harrison to deal with right now. Of course, the idea of a curse and a haunted desk was ridiculous! Still, he didn't relish starting the day with a major power struggle, so he decided to give Harrison the benefit of the doubt.

"There are no such things as ghosts and curses," said Mr.

Decker, "but if that seat makes you uncomfortable, we'll leave it empty for now. Take the front seat in the second row, Harrison."

"Thank you, Mr. Decker," said Harrison. He sat down in the front seat without another word, but his friends were certain Harrison had more disruption planned for later.

Mr. Decker took the opportunity to start the assignment for social studies.

"Please study the first chapter, class," he said. "We will be doing individual projects, so read the material carefully and think about what you'd like to do."

As his students opened their books, he began to make his lesson plans for the next day. He hadn't expected them to be so quiet. A silent alarm somewhere deep inside his brain went off. Too quiet! Too quiet! He glanced up and thought for a second that he saw a boy sitting in the last seat in the first row. He rubbed his hand across his eyes and saw that nobody was there, but he still felt uneasy.

Now they've got me believing in ghosts! he thought.

In the third seat in the first row, Aileen Beecher was feeling uneasy, too. She tried to concentrate on her reading, but a motion behind her was distracting her from her task. She looked over her shoulder at the last seat. Something had been there—she was sure of it! But whatever it was was gone by the time she focused on the chair. It was probably one of the other students trying to scare the class after Harrison's story.

Scared in School

She turned back to continue reading, but she could hear the soft swish of the custodian's mop in the hall near the classroom door. Aileen knew what he was cleaning up: she had seen a little first-grade boy cry and throw up when his mother had left him at school. Aileen knew how the little boy felt. She had wanted to do the same thing. Something about this school had made her stomach knot up as she came inside this morning. She felt no better now. She was glad that her brothers would be waiting to take her home after school.

Mr. Decker was relieved that no further problems developed during the morning. He wanted to get the year off to a good start.

At lunch, he saw some of his students giggling as they waited in line for their trays. He moved close enough to hear what they were saying, taking care that they didn't see him. Harrison was laughing loudest of all.

"I can't believe you told Mr. Decker that awful story," Candace said to Harrison. "You know Henry Huxley didn't put a curse on any desk before he died."

"That's right," said Annette. "That truck lost control and hit him, and he died instantly. He didn't have time to put a curse on anything even if he had wanted to!"

"If he could have cursed things," said Alan, "he wouldn't have wasted a curse on a desk! He would have cursed you for picking on him all the time!"

Harrison laughed. "He deserved to be picked on! He was a real wimp!"

So that's it! thought Mr. Decker. *I've got a first-rate bully and practical joker on my hands.*

Mr. Decker moved away from the students' line and joined some of the faculty at a nearby table.

"Was a student named Henry Huxley killed in an accident here last year?" he asked abruptly.

The teachers stopped eating. They all looked sad as they heard the little boy's name. Finally, one spoke.

"Yes, Henry was killed last year," she told Mr. Decker. "He was a nice little fellow. He loved school—that is, when the others weren't picking on him. Harrison Monroe gave him an especially hard time. Henry was playing ball with some of the kids after school when the driver of a delivery truck lost control. Harrison had just taunted Henry about missing the ball, so Henry had run onto the sidewalk to get it. The truck shot from the street and hit Henry. The poor child died instantly."

Mr. Decker listened intently as several others added details to the tragic story. His appetite had gone. He excused himself and slipped up to the classroom. He had a new lesson plan in mind just for Harrison. The class might enjoy a joke on Harrison Monroe for a change! He exchanged the seat in the back row with the one Harrison was using in front. Then smiling to himself, he returned to the cafeteria to escort his class back from lunch.

The students filed in and took their seats. Mr. Decker explained the math problems and allowed them to work until it was almost time for class to end.

"Class, please put your books away," said Mr. Decker. "I have something to tell you before you go."

Curious, the students quickly closed their books and waited.

"I learned at lunch that Harrison was telling the truth about Henry Huxley being killed," Mr. Decker continued.

Several students exchanged glances. They couldn't imagine what was coming.

"Harrison, how are you feeling sitting up front?" asked Mr. Decker.

"Fine, sir!" replied Harrison, beaming at the class.

"Good," said Mr. Decker. "We are all glad to hear that, I'm sure."

"Thank you, sir," said Harrison, grinning widely now as he enjoyed his joke.

"I learned something else at lunch, Harrison," continued Mr. Decker. "I learned that you were playing a distasteful joke on me. In case you convinced anyone in class that curses are real, I came up during lunch and arranged a little demonstration to prove that there is no such thing. You see, Harrison, I switched your desk with the one you said was cursed. You've been sitting in Henry's old seat since we came back from lunch, and yet you have just told all of us that you feel fine!"

Harrison Monroe's face turned fiery red, and the class roared with laughter.

"Let that be a lesson to you, Harrison," Mr. Decker laughed. "Don't be disrespectful to the dead by telling lies about them—and don't play jokes on your teacher."

The bell rang and Harrison ran from the room without a word.

"You got him good, Mr. Decker!" said Brett Burgess as he passed Mr. Decker's desk. "Nobody ever put one over on old Harrison before!"

Still, Mr. Decker felt terrible. Harrison hadn't taken the joke very well. He hadn't meant to humiliate the boy, but he had felt the boy needed to know what it was like to be on the receiving end of a practical joke. Harrison had been too upset to see the humor or the lesson when he ran from class. Mr. Decker made a mental note to apologize to Harrison in front of the entire class the next morning.

He sat at his desk a few minutes longer organizing the papers he wanted to take home to grade that night. He put them in his briefcase and walked to the front door to go home. He could see some boys playing ball on the sidewalk. He started to call to them to move back to the playground when a flash of blue swerved around the corner of 13th Street and Waiting Place. Mr.

Scared in School

Decker heard the screeching of brakes, followed by a loud crash, as teachers on bus duty turned and ran down the sidewalk.

Mr. Decker ran toward the accident, too. Neighbors came running out as students and teachers surrounded a still form on the concrete walk. Mr. Decker pushed his way through the crowd, but he knew who the victim was before he looked. It was Harrison Monroe, crushed beneath the wheels of the school board's blue delivery truck.

Aileen Beecher stood looking pale as death. She had sat in that seat for a few seconds before Harrison. Now he was dead. What would happen to her? she wondered. She heard Albert calling her name, but the sound seemed far away. She said nothing as he took her arm and led her away.

"Hurry!" he said. "I left my books in the computer lab."

Neither knew it was the last place they'd go together.

Extinguished Educators

The first day at 13th Street Middle School had not gone well for Bertha Stinson. She ran her stubby fingers through her short, curly gray hair and then pressed them against her temples. Her head throbbed. She stood outside the computer lab before her last class of the day wishing she didn't have to go in. She had never felt this way before in all of her twenty-seven years of teaching. It wasn't the students she dreaded, even though they were more unruly today than they had ever been on the first day in the past. It was the computers she dreaded. She wondered sometimes if Mr. Maxwell knew how much she disliked them and assigned her this class to force her to take early retirement. She was determined to do a good job just in case her suspicions were true.

She'd come in early and given instructions for her first class, but they had followed a completely different program. They all insisted they had followed the instructions on the screen. She was sure it was a prank, but she often felt the computers were in charge instead of her.

That was the feeling she'd gotten during her planning period when she'd gone to the lab for her papers. As she approached the lab door, she heard the familiar clacking of keyboards. She knew no class was scheduled for that time, so she threw open the door to catch the intruders. The room was empty.

She was amazed. She knew what she had heard, yet nobody was there now. There was no way out except through the door, and nobody had passed by her. She was sure she'd seen images fading from the screens. She ran her hand over the computers by the door, but they were cold and silent. She began to shiver. The room appeared empty, but Bertha could feel something menacing all around her. She snatched up her papers and ran.

Her first impulse was to tell someone immediately about her unnerving experience, but everybody around was busy. She wasn't going to interrupt any of her colleagues in their classes, that was for sure. They would think she was merely an old woman imagining things. She went to the lounge and graded her papers.

The rest of the day was uneventful, yet now she was in front of her classroom door shivering again. She smoothed her navy blue skirt and tugged at the matching vest she hoped would cover the roundness in her belly. She forced herself to enter and begin the lesson. On the surface everything seemed normal, but something was stirring beneath the outward calm. She saw the students give her puzzled glances as she hurried them through their lessons, but she didn't care. She only cared about the class ending and the children leaving. When the final bell rang, she shooed them out as quickly as possible. After they'd gone, she noticed that in the rush, Albert Beecher had left his books.

"No problem," she said to herself as she locked the lab door behind her. "He probably won't miss them until tomorrow."

Bertha Stinson was wrong about there being no problem.

She was hurrying across the parking lot to her car when she heard the screech of brakes by the elementary school. She ran like the others to see Harrison Monroe's crushed body. Her fear today must have been a premonition of this tragedy—she had had other premonitions on occasion—but the fear continued to nag her as she made her way to the parking lot. She did not see Albert lead Aileen away to get his books.

Brian Beecher did see them, though. He had been in the hall by the third floor window when he heard the crash. His heart missed a beat when he realized a boy had been hit. His feet barely touched the steps as he raced down the two flights and out the door. He thought at first it was Albert when he saw Aileen's frozen stare from the sidewalk.

"Get back!" a voice told him. "Get back!"

Brian pushed against the body that blocked him.

"My brother—" he gasped, struggling.

Then he had seen Albert touch Aileen's arm and lead her toward the middle school.

Brian jerked loose from the guard and ran to the corner.

Scared in School

He watched Albert and Aileen turn up the walk. The traffic light held red. He called for them to wait, but his voice couldn't compete with the wail of sirens. He saw them enter the building as the light turned green. He stepped from the curb, but stopped short as an ambulance and police car zoomed by. Like the other spectators, he stood silently while the little boy was lifted onto the stretcher and covered. The siren was silent now. The wailing would come from living things.

Brian crossed to the middle school. Nobody was in the office, so Brian walked down the hall. He saw Mr. Maxwell, the principal, and the custodian talking in low voices by the computer lab.

"Excuse me," said Brian as he approached. "I'm Brian Beecher. I'm looking for my brother Albert and my sister Aileen."

Mr. Maxwell and the custodian exchanged glances.

"Come to my office with me, son," said Mr. Maxwell. "We seem to have a problem."

"Have they done something, sir?" asked Brian.

"Yes, son, I am afraid they have. They've disappeared!"

The next hours were a continuing nightmare. Brian allowed Mr. Maxwell to guide him to the office. He listened while Mr. Maxwell phoned his mother and told her that Albert and Aileen had gone into the computer lab and never come out. The two children had come in to get some books Albert had left. Mr. Maxwell had directed the custodian to unlock the door for them. The two men had stood talking outside in the hall while the children went in. When they didn't come out, Mr. Maxwell went to the door and called to them. Getting no response, the two men had become concerned and gone inside the lab to look for them. Nobody was there! The lab had no windows, and neither man had seen the children leave through the door. They had vanished without a clue! Mr. Maxwell and the custodian had just completed a second search when Brian walked up.

Brian went to the lab and looked for himself. When his mother arrived, he tried to comfort her. They must have slipped by the men in the hall unnoticed and gone to try to find Brian. He left his mom crying into Mr. Maxwell's white cotton handkerchief and went to look at the bus stop and the other schools. There was not a trace!

"We'll find them, Mom," he told her when he came back to take her home, but deep down he wasn't sure. He hoped his words would comfort her, though.

That evening, Bertha Stinson fixed herself a chicken pot pie and ate it on a TV tray as she watched the news. It had become a ritual since her husband had died the year before. She was still fighting a sense of dread when the anchorman's reference to 13th Street School brought her to attention. She had expected to hear about Harrison Monroe, but she had to steady herself by grabbing her tray when she heard about the missing Beecher children.

Scared in School

Two missing, one dead, she thought.

As she listened to the report, she chided herself for thinking such a phrase. She'd thought of them as if they were casualties of war.

There was still no word on the missing children in the morning. Bertha Stinson went to school wondering if she ought to say something to the principal about her odd experience in the lab. She wondered if something like that had happened to the children and if it could be connected in some way to their disappearance. She decided against saying anything. What she was thinking was impossible. Besides, she had only three more years before she could retire and she'd already overheard a few remarks that she was getting too old to teach. If she said anything, everybody would think she didn't like to teach computers because she was too set in her ways. If she tried to connect the computers to the missing children, they would think she was crazy or senile. She was still thinking about it when Mr. Maxwell called her to his office.

"Great news, Mrs. Stinson!" he told her. "You're getting two new experimental computers for your lab."

"How nice," she said, managing to smile.

"Yes," agreed Mr. Maxwell. "A company called KnowKids has donated them. Catchy name, huh?"

Bertha smiled and nodded.

"They say they will donate more later if these work out,"

Mr. Maxwell continued. "We'll have these two set up by tomorrow. I want you to use them and report back to me on how well they do."

"I will, sir," said Bertha. "It was very generous of the company to do this for us."

"Yes, indeed," beamed Mr. Maxwell. "They even gave me one for my office."

Bertha Stinson walked by it as she left the office. She felt a faint prickling under her skin until she was out the door.

The new computers were in place the next morning. The students accepted them like old friends, but Bertha tingled when she came near them.

"These are compatible with our other computers," said David Palmer. "Isn't that great, Mrs. Stinson?"

"Great," she agreed.

She had to admit they worked beautifully. She tried to find something negative to say about them in her report, but she kept coming up blank. Her late husband had always told her not to look for trouble. This might be a time to take his advice.

For the next few days, Bertha Stinson tried to be positive. The last hour on Thursday was the worst. The class entered the room chasing each other, bumping chairs as they sat down, and throwing strips from the edges of old printouts like they were confetti. The computers sat silent like sentinels. Bertha wondered what secrets they were guarding. Then she wondered if she had gone crazy or grown senile or a little of both.

"Computers are just machines," she reminded herself sternly. "I've got to get my class begun and forget this nonsense. I can't imagine what's the matter with me."

Bertha Stinson cleared her throat and waited, but nobody heard her.

"Good morning, class," she said. "May I have your attention?"

Again nobody heard or responded.

"Class, be quiet!" she shouted.

The noise stopped abruptly, and they all turned to look at her. Two timid girls looked upset by her shouting and shrank back into their seats.

She opened her mouth to apologize to the class, but she was interrupted by the sound of the printer starting up beside her. The class stared at her and she stared at the class. Then they all stared at the printer until it stopped.

For a moment, nobody moved. Then David Palmer stood up and started toward the printer.

"No!" shrieked Mrs. Stinson.

Startled by the outburst from his teacher, David sat back down. Bertha Stinson was startled, too. She hadn't intended to yell like that. She had felt that David was in danger, but of course she couldn't tell the class that. They were already puzzled by her actions.

"I'm sorry, class," she said, tearing off the printout and folding it to fit into her pocket. "I'm a little jumpy today. Let's get on with our work so I can give Mr. Maxwell a good report on our new computers."

Bertha held the folded paper in her pocket. Reluctantly, the students turned to their assignments. Bertha caught them watching her when they thought she wasn't looking. She didn't care what they thought. She didn't know what to think about the printer. If this was a trick they were playing on her, she wouldn't give them the satisfaction of letting them see her read the message.

She could feel the folded paper in her pocket as she went about teaching the class for the rest of the period. She forced herself to leave it there after school while she shopped at the market, prepared dinner, and ate.

After dinner, she considered going to a movie, but she saw that it had begun to rain. She didn't like driving in the rain at night, so she tried to think of something else to take her mind off the printout. She knew she must read it sooner or later, but she sensed that when she did, her life would somehow be changed forever.

She could find no more excuses for putting it off. She pulled it slowly from her pocket and unfolded it. She sat at her desk and turned on the reading lamp. With trembling hands, she held the paper under the light and read the message.

Scared in School

When she finished, her heart was racing. She tried to think what to do, but her thoughts were jumbled. Should she call Mr. Maxwell at home? No, she couldn't do that. He'd think she was insane. The students would verify it after her behavior in class today. Mr. Maxwell couldn't do anything anyway. It was the police she needed. With a trembling hand, she called a cab. She read the message again while she waited by the door.

The rain had not let up, but Bertha Stinson hardly noticed as she rode in the cab to the police station. She had thought of calling the police since she was too upset to drive, but she had decided it was worth paying for a cab to show them the message in person. She would seem like less of a kook that way.

The police station was nearly deserted when Bertha paid the cabby and burst through the station door, wild-eyed and dripping with rain.

"I know where the missing children are!" she told the officer at the desk. "You know, the Beecher children from my school! Read this printout! It will explain everything."

The officer led Bertha to a chair and spent several minutes calming her down before he read the paper she had thrust at him when she entered. He read the message and noticed Bertha shaking uncontrollably.

"Take it easy, lady," the officer said. "Take a deep breath and tell me your name."

"Bertha Stinson," she said, still trembling.

The officer looked at the piece of paper again. "Mrs. Stinson," he said. "I'm afraid this doesn't make much sense to me. Maybe you can clarify a few things." He read the message aloud this time.

WE ARE PART OF AN OUTER SPACE PROGRAM. "NOKIDS" IS OUR LATEST PROJECT. WE TURN KIDS INTO COMPUTERS. WE HAVE STARTED WITH YOUR SCHOOL, BUT WE WILL TAKE OVER THE WORLD. BEWARE! THERE WILL BE MORE.

"Don't you see?" asked Bertha. "The little Beecher children disappeared in the computer lab. The space people turned them into computers. I'm sure the kids sent this message for help. What are you going to do about it?"

At that point, the officer at the desk called his captain. Bertha watched their short consultation. She saw the captain pick up the telephone and call Mr. Maxwell. He agreed to meet them at the school immediately.

"An officer will escort Mrs. Stinson over right away," said the captain.

"Thank you," said Mr. Maxwell. "I think it's best to settle this before the students arrive in the morning."

Bertha was calm on the ride to school. Whatever happened now would not be on her conscience. She had done her duty.

Scared in School

Mr. Maxwell listened with concern as the officer related the night's events and Bertha's theory about the missing children. Mr. Maxwell patted Bertha's shoulder when the officer finished.

"I'm afraid the students have played a cruel trick on you, Mrs. Stinson," he explained. "Kids today are whizzes at computers. They've altered the introductory message on the new computers. Here, let me show you. This computer they gave me is identical to the new ones in your lab."

Mr. Maxwell turned on his computer and pulled up the introductory message. He directed Bertha and the officer to look at the screen as he read the message aloud.

WE ARE PART OF AN OUTREACH PROGRAM. "KNOWKIDS" IS OUR LATEST PROJECT. WE TURN KIDS ALL OVER THE WORLD INTO COMPUTER EXPERTS. WE HAVE STARTED WITH TWO COMPUTERS AT YOUR SCHOOL. WE WILL SOON PROVIDE MORE.

Mr. Maxwell pushed a key and the image faded.

"No!" cried Bertha. "I tell you, these computers are dangerous! They're evil! You've got to get rid of them before they destroy us all!"

The officer, standing behind Bertha, shook his head at Mr. Maxwell. This wasn't teacher burn-out. It was flip-out!

"Mrs. Stinson, I'm sorry the students upset you," said Mr.

Maxwell. "I'll deal with them as soon as they come in. I am going to arrange for you to take some time off and rest. I want you to go home now. I'll call your doctor."

"I'll take her home," offered the officer.

As soon as they were out of the office, Mr. Maxwell switched on his computer. He typed in the file name NOKIDS and smiled to himself. Soon the project would be completed. The children would become the computer force to control this planet. Without offspring, the human race would soon be wiped out. The free thinkers, the nonconformists, or those who got in the way by accident would have to be dealt with like dirt disappearing with the swish of a custodian's mop!

Mr. Maxwell opened his filing cabinet and took out Bertha Stinson's folder. He studied it and entered all the pertinent information in the new computer. Then he punched the command key marked PAUSE.

Across town, Bertha was resting in bed after taking the sedative her doctor gave her, and in that instant, her life on earth as she had known it was deleted like an empty screen.

Student Bodies

On the second day of school, Kirk was at the bus stop early. Phil Yates slowed his large black car when he saw Kirk on the sidewalk, but he quickly drove on when he saw Kirk's mother bringing Kirk the lunch he'd forgotten.

Something weird is going on with that guy, thought Kirk.

Everything went smoothly for Kirk that second day. The bus was on time, Russell told funny jokes, and the rain that was forecast again held off so they could play ball outside during P.E. class.

"Nobody picked Karen," Russell pointed out. "She's such a loser."

Kirk saw her standing alone as the game began. He felt sorry for her. When Kirk looked up later, he saw her walking away with Mr. Yates.

On the third day of school, Kirk waited inside until he saw Mr. Yates drive by. It was nice that the counselor was taking so much time for Karen, but still, Kirk couldn't shake off the creepy impression he'd gotten when Mr. Yates had offered him a ride that first morning. After Mr. Yates's car slowed and passed, Kirk raced to the bus stop. He exchanged nods with the driver and took his usual seat in the back.

Neither Russell nor Karen were at their stops, but Kirk didn't think that was odd. He knew Russell's mother was taking him to the dentist, and she would drop him off at school later. Karen had often missed school last year to take care of her grandmother.

In homeroom, the teacher handed Kirk a note.

"Mr. Yates wants to see you in his office now," she said.

Kirk took the note and walked slowly down the hall.

The door was open when Kirk reached the office. Mr. Yates was sitting behind his desk studying a file.

"Excuse me, sir," said Kirk. "Did you want to see me?"

"Yes, Kirk," said Mr. Yates. "Please come in and close the door."

Kirk did as he was told, but he didn't feel comfortable as he pulled the door closed behind him.

"Did I do something wrong?" asked Kirk.

"No, of course not," said Mr. Yates. "Sit down. I need to talk to you about something confidential. Do you promise not to tell anyone?"

"Yeah," replied Kirk, puzzled by Mr. Yates's question.

"I know you think it's strange that I've driven by your house every morning. I think I may have even frightened you a little," said Mr. Yates. "I feel I owe you an explanation. I could also use your help."

"Sure," said Kirk, beginning to feel more at ease as he

waited for Mr. Yates to continue.

"When Karen came in before school to register for class-es, she told me a man had been following her. Then when she rode the bus, she recognized the man. She said it was your new bus driver. She also said he might have been one of her mother's old boyfriends."

Mr. Yates paused and waited for Kirk's reaction.

"Karen's always saying someone is weird," said Kirk. "I don't know about her mother's boyfriends. She had a lot of them, if you know what I mean. It was hard on Karen when her mom died. I sort of know how she feels. My dad died a couple of years ago."

Kirk knew he was talking too much. He wished Mr. Yates would say something to interrupt, but he only nodded as Kirk finished. A moment passed before he spoke.

"I'm having a background check done on the bus driver," confided Mr. Yates. "While I'm waiting for the report, I've been driving along the bus route to make sure everything is alright. You, Russell, and Karen are the ones I am most concerned about since you are more isolated than the other students. They can wait at the bus stop in groups, but the three of you wait alone. You are alone with the driver for seven blocks, so anything could happen."

"Oh," said Kirk, relieved at the explanation.

The new driver certainly was a mystery. He never talked

to the students like the old driver did.

"I hope I haven't frightened you," said Mr. Yates.

"Oh, no," lied Kirk.

"Good," said Mr. Yates. "I thought you were mature enough to handle this."

"Sure," said Kirk, feeling more grown-up than he'd ever felt in his life.

"Let me know if the driver does anything unusual," said Mr. Yates, "and I'll let you know what I find out."

"Thanks, Mr. Yates," said Kirk, standing up to go. "I'm glad you told me."

Kirk hurried back to class. He wished he could tell Russell about his talk with Mr. Yates, but he knew he couldn't. Russell would tell. Kirk knew it would have to be his secret for now.

Homeroom was over, so Kirk went directly to P.E. class for first period. He stopped inside the gym and looked around, surprised that the class was sitting quietly on the floor. Coach Richards looked upset, so Kirk sat down quietly with the other students. He looked around for Russell, but he wasn't there. He must have been delayed at the dentist.

"Boys and girls, I have some terrible news to tell you," the coach began. "I want you to know that all the staff will be here to help you deal with this."

Coach Richards paused to get control of himself before

he continued.

"Something horrible happened last night. Karen Frazier was murdered."

The entire class gasped in unison.

"The killer left her body in the vacant lot behind the Newmans' house." The coach's voice broke here, but he made himself go on. "Russell and his mother found Karen this morning when they were going to the dentist."

Kirk sat stunned. He could hear some of the girls sobbing softly.

"For your own safety, we decided to tell you the truth," said the coach. "I know this is shocking, but this killer could still be around. You must use caution. Be alert until he is caught."

Kirk saw that Mr. Yates had joined the coach in front of the class now. His face looked white and strained.

"I just heard what happened," Mr. Yates told the group. "I have called for extra grief counselors to come in to talk to you. Of course, I will be available to do all I can. This is a terrible tragedy, but we'll get through it together."

Kirk didn't know if he could get through the next hour. Things like this only happened in other places. This couldn't be happening in this school to someone he knew! He went to his classes, but all the talk was about the murder. It was the same when he got home. The murder was covered on every newscast.

Kirk tried calling Russell, but his mother said the doctor

had given him something to make him sleep. She said that he wouldn't be going to school the next day. Seeing Karen's body had been a tremendous shock.

Kirk's mother knew he was upset, too, and she was afraid for him to stay home alone. Even though she knew she would be late for work, she waited with him at the bus stop the next morning. Kirk wanted to tell her that Mr. Yates was suspicious of the bus driver, but he'd more or less promised he wouldn't say anything. He dreaded the seven-block ride alone.

Headlights turned the corner, and Kirk watched them come down the street. He'd have to get on the bus. His mother would think he was nuts if he told her he was afraid of the driver. He turned to get his bookbag, but his mother tugged at his arm.

"Come on," she said. "That's not the school bus."

Kirk looked around as the large black car pulled up to the curb and stopped.

"Come on!" his mother repeated more urgently.

"It's OK, Mom," Kirk told her. "That's Mr. Yates, my counselor."

"After what's happened, I thought you might want a ride to school, Kirk," called Mr. Yates as he rolled down the window.

"Can I, Mom?" asked Kirk.

"That would be great!" said his mother. "I'm already late for work."

Kirk opened the door, threw his bookbag on the seat, and

climbed in. He waved at his mom as Mr. Yates pulled away. He tried not to look at the vacant lot behind Russell's house as they drove by, but he couldn't help himself. The police were still out there digging.

"The news said some of Karen's things are missing," Kirk said as they turned the corner.

"Yes, I heard," said Mr. Yates. "Her diary and her purse, according to her grandmother."

The vacant lot was far behind them now, but Kirk's thoughts were still back there. When the car bumped across the railroad tracks, it jolted Kirk back to the present. He saw that they were now on a street near the river. They were nowhere near the school.

"You took a wrong turn back there, Mr. Yates," said Kirk. "We're going in the wrong direction."

"Really?" said Mr. Yates. "Well, you know how easy it is to get lost when you are in a new place."

"If you turn right at the next light, we'll be headed in the direction we want to go," said Kirk.

At the light, Mr. Yates made a left turn.

"I said you needed to turn right to get where you want to go," said Kirk.

"I am going where I want to go," said Mr. Yates. "Relax."

He was smiling at Kirk again, but only with his mouth. Kirk had never been less relaxed in his life. It all came to him in a flash.

"You made up that stuff about the bus driver, didn't you, Mr. Yates?" Kirk asked. He'd meant to sound strong and brave, but his voice came out in a whisper. "You killed her!"

Mr. Yates didn't answer. He kept the smile on his face and his eyes focused on the street.

Panic gave Kirk his voice back.

"Let me out!" he screamed. "Stop the car right now!"

A narrow paved street led from the main street down toward the river. Beyond the riverbank, the woods loomed. Mr. Yates pulled onto the narrow street and stopped. Everything was deserted. He cut off the engine and turned toward Kirk.

Kirk grabbed the door handle, but the door was locked. He shook it frantically, but it wouldn't budge. All he did was knock his bookbag off the seat. It landed on his foot and the pain made him realize the bag would be a good weapon. As he reached down for it, he saw the edge of something pink sticking out from under the seat. He knew he had seen it before. It was Karen's diary! He pulled it out, but he was not prepared for what came with it. The screams rose one after another from his throat as he saw Karen Frazier's fingernail stuck in her diary at that last entry.

Mr. Yates laughed. He made no move to stop Kirk as he picked it up. "Read it if you like," said Mr. Yates. "It's not true. It didn't happen that way."

Scared in School

Kirk's screams had subsided now to a gurgle of terror. Russell had read the first words when Karen dropped the diary on the bus: *"At orientation last week, the new counselor ..."*

Kirk remembered that Karen had finished the entry as they rode to school. Kirk read what she had written.

"At orientation last week, the new counselor touched me and made me do things too bad to write about. He warned me that he'd kill me if I told. I told my grandmother, anyway, but she didn't believe me. Nobody else will believe me either, but I've got to do something about that awful man. I can't stand for him to put his hands on me again!"

Kirk stopped reading and looked accusingly at Mr. Yates.

"I never meant to kill her," Mr. Yates said softly, reaching for Kirk's arm. "We needed to examine her, but she wouldn't go to the light with me. You won't resist, will you, Kirk?"

"You're crazy," Kirk said, pulling away. "Leave me alone!"

"Cooperate and you won't get hurt," said Mr. Yates.

Karen was right about this guy, and so was I, Kirk thought, *but what's good about being right if you're dead?*

Mr. Yates's right hand shot out and clamped on the back of Kirk's head. Mr. Yates took a black case from his shirt pocket with his other hand. He placed it on his lap and flipped it open. Kirk saw a small shiny object like a cigar. Mr. Yates turned Kirk's head to the left. He took the object from the case and began moving it back and forth in front of Kirk's eyes. Light glowed in a circle.

"Relax," he ordered. "You will remember nothing."

Kirk felt himself getting sleepy.

"Relax," Mr. Yates repeated.

Kirk's eyelids fluttered open. His vision was blurred. He didn't want to sleep, but it was easier than fighting the drowsiness. A floating sensation filled Kirk's body as Mr. Yates lifted and carried him into the dense woods. He forced himself to open his eyes. He saw a huge silver cylindrical spaceship reaching to the treetops. It was like the miniature one Mr. Yates had moved back and forth before his eyes. Kirk thought it was strange to see one of it when he was seeing two of Mr. Yates's head.

"Sleep," Mr. Yates commanded.

Kirk obeyed. His eyes automatically closed. He was drunk now, spinning into darkness.

When he awoke, he felt confused. Had he been dreaming? He didn't think so. The silver cylinder had been real, but the image was fading now. Faces and objects were coming into focus. He realized that he was in Mr. Yates's office, and he saw his mother, Mr. Yates, and Mr. Maxwell looking down at him on the couch. He tried to sit up, but he felt groggy.

"What happened?" he asked his mom.

"Mr. Yates said you were talking about Karen and you fainted in the car. He brought you here and called me," she explained.

Scared in School

"But I've never fainted before," Kirk said.

"No friend of yours has ever been murdered either," she said.

"Death has strange effects," Mr. Maxwell added.

"Yeah, I guess so," Kirk agreed.

He sat up on the couch and rubbed his neck. His fingers stopped on a small cut on his hairline. He was sure it hadn't been there before. He must have hit something when he fainted.

"How do you feel, Kirk?" asked Mr. Yates, his eyes locking Kirk's.

Kirk felt sore and stiff, as if he'd been poked and probed. But when he tried to speak, the words wouldn't come out.

"I'm fine," he heard himself saying. "I'd like to go now."

As his mother helped him from the couch, he wanted to believe he was fine. There were two problems, though. First, he had no memory from the time he got into Mr. Yates's car until he woke up in the office. And second, when his mother led him out the door, he could have sworn that Mr. Yates had two heads.

Dead Ahead

News of the missing Beecher children was now replaced by headlines of Karen Frazier's murder. Brian had been shocked that he had known all the people who had been the focus of the evening news in the last few days. Then the doorbell had rung and Brian was more shocked than ever. His mother had opened the door to find his father standing there. She had actually let him in after all he'd done.

He lay on his bed now in the dark feeling hurt and angry as the voices of his mother and father drifted up from the kitchen.

I wish I had answered the door tonight, thought Brian. *I would have kicked Dad's butt out in the street.*

He knew he could have done it, too. His father had lost weight while Brian had filled out and developed muscles. He couldn't believe his mom had been so glad to see his father.

"When I heard about Albert and Aileen, I had to come back," his dad had told her. "I couldn't let you and Brian go through this alone."

He held out his arms and she fell right into them.

Brian had cursed under his breath and bolted for his room.

Scared in School

"Brian, come back!" his mother had called after him.

"Let him go," he heard his father say. "He needs some time."

Brian had no idea of how little time he had as he lay on the bed going over the events of the last few weeks. First, that Monroe kid had been hit by the delivery truck. Funny, the spokesman for the board of education said the truck was at the 13th Street Elementary School by mistake. A computer error sent it to the wrong place! Then Albert and Aileen had disappeared in a computer lab. David Palmer had told Brian how odd the computer lab's teacher had acted the day before she took early retirement. He had been sure that these happenings were somehow connected to the computers until Karen Frazier's murder. Computers didn't use knives to carve up victims.

"This place is evil," his mother had sobbed earlier that night as they watched the news. "We'd move now, but I can't go until I am sure Albert and Aileen are not here somewhere."

"Where would we go?" asked Brian.

"I don't know," she answered. "I've thought about it, but evil is everywhere these days. And it comes in all forms, Brian."

Brian had turned off the television and was thinking about Karen. Just then the doorbell had rung.

"I'll get it," she said, hurrying to answer it. "Maybe it's news about Albert and Aileen."

She's still hoping, thought Brian.

His mother turned the key and pulled the door wide open before Brian could move. She gasped and clung to the door when she saw her husband. Then he held out his arms to her and she'd fallen into them.

When Brian saw his father standing there, he thought she was right. This place was evil. Now in the early hours of morning, he was more sure!

His parents had finally gone to bed, but Brian couldn't sleep. He got up to close the curtains to see if that would help, but a bright flash of light caught his eye. It came up from the direction of the woods behind the school and disappeared so quickly he questioned whether he saw it at all. He thought of UFOs again. Surely he hadn't seen one of them.

He did see his father's car parked by the curb, though. He thought about the promise his dad had made to get him a car for his sixteenth birthday and an idea came to his mind. He could take the car for a quick spin, maybe to the woods where he'd seen the light. He opened the bedroom door and closed it softly behind him. He tiptoed down the stairs, taking special care not to step on the creaky board near the hall table. His father used to leave his car keys by the door. Tonight was no exception. Brian picked them up and slipped out. As he got behind the wheel, he no longer felt like a frightened boy. Tonight he was a man.

Five o'Clock Feedings

Rain began to fall as Brian sped toward the woods. He could see a circle of light above the trees. He turned on the wipers and dropped his speed somewhat. His extra care didn't matter, though. Evil was waiting for him.

It lay quietly stretched out in the pre-dawn darkness, its white and yellow markings exposed to the rain. It had welcomed the collision of the deer and the young man's car. It could feel the blood of its five o'clock feeding soaking through its pores along with the raindrops. It was full and replenished now. It would not bother the others that went by.

Today the deer and the young man had been an unexpected feast. Pickings were usually slim at five A.M., but it waited anyway. Sometimes it paid off like this morning, but usually more choices popped up in the evenings. It only had to lie still.

Some travelers went along and never noticed it. A few were uncaring, though, and knocked chunks out of its smooth, dark surface. These were the ones it remembered.

When the hunger became too great, anything would do. It couldn't go looking for food, so it took the first thing that came by. That was the case today with the man and the deer.

The man was innocent enough. He had never been this

way before, so he had done no harm. Unfortunately, he had come along when the belly was empty and rumbling to be filled. The young man was guilty only of bad timing.

It felt badly about the deer and had tried to apologize in its own way, but the deer was dead instantly. It would not have taken the deer's life if it hadn't needed the young man.

It understood how the deer felt. Like the deer, it had been driven from its natural habitat by men and, like the deer, it had nowhere else to go. There was only the difference of mobility. It had no feet with which to run like the deer. It could only wait for its food to come to it. It wished it could move about and be more selective. It got tired of food from metal containers.

The blood and flesh of the deer had been a delicacy, but it would never seek out animals for food. It shared with them the common bond of hatred for human beings.

For years, humans had put it and others like it in every conceivable place. It and the others were left to endure the snow of mountains or the heat of deserts. Humans left them alone in the country or put them down in the midst of busy city traffic. The humans never considered whether they wanted to be there or not.

Humans always acted superior. Few read the warning signs of trouble and heeded them, but they would pay for their ignorance and arrogance. It would make them pay.

It watched silently as men, sad but efficient as custodians, came in the rain and removed the remains of the man and the deer.

"Look at the blood they lost," one said.

The blood was not lost, though. It had filled the empty belly and stopped the rumbling temporarily.

People passed the scene of the five o'clock feeding filled with relief that they were not the ones involved.

As the days passed, people forgot. They whizzed by, not hearing the ominous rumblings signaling that the empty belly was ready for another meal.

Five o'clock traffic jammed lanes bumper to bumper heading home. A large truck turned onto the entrance ramp, and the pavement buckled under the load. The trucker fought for control, but the truck barreled into the lane of traffic.

Blood from the broken bodies soaked into the super highway, and the rumblings beneath it stopped. The metal from the cars that had carried its dinner lay scattered and shining like tin cans in the afternoon sun.

While the highway lay full and satisfied, a few lucky travelers were able to slip safely by it to happier destinations. It didn't mind. Others were sure to come along in time for its next five o'clock feeding. Brian's father—on his way out of town again—would be one.

Ghoul School

The holidays were approaching and those in the schools on 13th Street tried to put their tragic memories behind them and make plans for the rest of the year.

Kirk Radborne's microchip settled into place at the base of his skull. He felt a twinge in his neck from time to time, but he had no idea why. He only knew that the twinge brought light circles and thoughts to his mind that were not his own. He had no resistance to whatever the thoughts told him to do.

Mrs. Rutherford wished the stray cat she'd found was black. Snowball wouldn't be very frightening for Halloween, but she hoped she would give the classroom a little atmosphere and help out with the mouse problem.

Nathan Gaylord had two problems. One was his dad and Greta Parks and the other was his science project that was due before Thanksgiving. The thing that he was most grateful for was that he possibly had a solution for both.

As winter temperatures set in, Addie Forest didn't want to drive downtown to the YWCA in the snow. Instead, she moved her physical fitness program to the school halls, where she took her daily walks.

Right after Christmas, Hobert Burton and Josh Morgan began

to dream of baseball. Kevin Hale transferred to 13th Street Middle School.

By the end of school, Miss Payne was reconsidering her discipline procedures and her role in extracurricular activities.

"Surely nothing else can happen this year," they said.

It was the wrong thing to say.

———————————————

Science Slab

Robert Harrison was enjoying his science class at 13th Street Middle School until his teacher, Mrs. Rutherford, brought that stray cat to school. He couldn't believe that the principal would allow a cat to live in the school building!

"Snowball is only here for a little while so we can observe her," said Mrs. Rutherford, rubbing her red, chubby cheek against Snowball's fur. "We're having trouble getting rid of the mice in the storage room, so Snowball will earn her keep by catching them."

Snowball, Mrs. Rutherford called her. The cat's sleek, white hair didn't make Robert think of anything as pure and lovely as snow. Robert associated cats with the coldness of death. He still remembered how a cat had smothered his baby sister. He knew it was supposed to be an old wives' tale about cats sucking the breath out of babies, but he knew it had happened with his sister. The doctor had called it a crib death, but Robert had seen the cat jump from the crib and escape through the window. It had looked at him with triumph in its eyes as it paused on the window sill. Robert had realized the cat was jealous of the baby, but his mom and dad wouldn't listen. They had told Robert that he was the jealous one!

After the death of his sister, the cat was restored to its place as King of the Household. His parents pampered it, but Robert avoided it. He made sure the door to his room was locked every night before he went to sleep.

Then one day, much to Robert's delight, the cat came up missing. Two days later, a neighbor found the cat in a ditch by the side of the road. It had been struck and killed by a car. Robert's mother cried, but Robert felt nothing except relief. He didn't want to admit it, but he was afraid of cats and he never wanted another one around. He'd been lucky until Snowball appeared outside the school and Mrs. Rutherford made her a resident of Room 205!

Snowball sensed immediately that Robert was an enemy. She purred when Kirk Radborne held her, and she allowed the other students to pet her. But she hissed and ran for the storage room when Robert came near.

You don't have to worry, you stupid cat, thought Robert. *I have no intention of petting you!*

"Try to make friends with her, Robert," Mrs. Rutherford coaxed.

"Sure, Mrs. Rutherford," agreed Robert, but he made no effort to get close to the cat.

Robert could have tolerated Snowball in the class if she had continued to keep her distance, but she didn't. As she gained confidence about her position in the classroom, she zeroed in on Robert's desk for mischief. Each day she did something annoying or destructive.

First, it was dead mice. Robert had placed his lunch beside his seat one day like he always did, but when he reached down to pick up the brown paper lunch bag, he touched something furry instead. He jumped and jerked his hand back. When he looked to see what it was, he had seen the two dead mice resting against his lunch bag.

As Robert jumped to his feet, turning his chair over by his abrupt movement, he heard a low purring, almost like a laugh, coming from Snowball.

"You hateful cat!" Robert shouted.

Everyone in the classroom, including Mrs. Rutherford, turned to stare at Robert and then at the mice.

Some of the girls screamed and some of the boys laughed. Kirk Radborne's eyes followed the cat. Mrs. Rutherford quickly took control of the situation.

"Now, Robert, calm down," she said. "Snowball is only trying to get your attention. You never pet her like the others do."

Robert was paying no attention to Mrs. Rutherford. He had moved around his overturned chair and was moving slowly, menacingly toward Snowball.

"Meow!" she howled as he approached, and she dashed for the safety of the storage room.

Robert was intent on following when the sharp voice of Mrs. Rutherford stopped him.

"Return to your seat this very instant and leave Snowball alone," she ordered. "Take some paper and wrap those mice and then remove them from class."

"Me?" objected Robert. "Why should I carry the dead mice out? She dragged them in here."

"I will tolerate no back talk from you, young man," said Mrs. Rutherford. "You will do as you're told at once. Now remove the mice so we can go to lunch."

Kirk felt the twinge in the back of his neck. Thoughts came from the microchip: *We have plans for you. You must be kind now so nobody will suspect you when the time comes to put our plan into action.*

Kirk left his seat and knelt by Robert's desk. He wrapped the mice in notebook paper and held them up to Robert. Robert took the mice and left the room, carrying the dead rodents to their dumpster tomb.

"Thanks, man," he whispered to Kirk when he returned a few minutes later. Kirk smiled and nodded.

Snowball, secure now in the safety offered by her champion, Mrs. Rutherford, began a daily ritual of pouncing on Robert's desk during class. The result was always disastrous. Homework papers were knocked to the floor, test tubes were broken, and any liquid in the vicinity was spilled on the desk or the floor.

Scared in School

Whenever anything happened involving Snowball, Robert lost no time complaining to Mrs. Rutherford. Her response was never sympathetic. She'd hold Snowball and stroke her, while Snowball would purr and look innocent.

"See?" Mrs. Rutherford would say. "Snowball wouldn't hurt a fly. You're clumsy and you're trying to blame Snowball for your problem."

Snowball would concur with a pitiful meow.

Little by little, the other students in class with the exception of Kirk began to side with Snowball, agreeing that all the disruptions were indeed Robert's fault, and that Robert was being unreasonable and unfair to pick on the poor cat!

Meanwhile, Snowball continued to run free in the classroom and to pillage through Robert's personal property. On several occasions, Robert caught her playing with pens on his desk or pawing at the aquarium when no one else was looking. When Robert would start toward her, she would move quickly to avoid his clutches, lingering just long enough to let him know that she was enjoying their undeclared war.

Snowball was a master at coming from her hiding places and running between Robert's feet. Once, she tripped him in front of the whole class. Kirk helped him up, but the students' laughter rang in Robert's ears for days. He vowed to get rid of Snowball if it was the last thing he ever did.

The next morning, Robert came to school early. The door

to the science room was open as usual, and Mrs. Rutherford was down the hall talking to Mrs. Herbert, the art teacher. Robert ducked inside without being seen. He looked around, but Snowball was nowhere in sight. He reached inside his pocket and pulled out the container of tuna he'd poisoned that morning before leaving for school.

"Here, kitty, kitty," he called softly.

Suddenly, from the top of one of the cabinets, Snowball pounced on top of Robert's head. Startled, Robert let go of the tuna container and grabbed for the cat. Snowball leapt gracefully to the floor and approached the container that had lost its cover in the fall.

Snowball sniffed the tuna and stared at Robert with a look that said, *Really, now! What do you take me for?*

She started walking toward the storage room door, but when she got even with Robert she stopped and lunged at him with a loud hiss. Robert swung his notebook and sent the cat flying against the wall. Snowball fell to the floor and did not move so much as a whisker.

Robert retrieved the lid to the container, snapped it in place, and returned the container to his pocket. The dreadful creature still wasn't moving. He hadn't meant to kill her this way. He had hoped she'd eat the rat poison in the tuna and that everybody would think she had somehow gotten contaminated food from school's trash dumpster.

Scared in School

He tried to think what to do now. He couldn't let Mrs. Rutherford know what had really happened. She'd flunk him and maybe even have him suspended or arrested! He'd have to hide Snowball in the storage room and then sneak out of the room before Mrs. Rutherford came back.

Robert had never handled a dead cat before. *Gross,* he thought, leaning over Snowball to pick her up.

At the first touch, Snowball's eyes opened, her fur stood on end, her tail swished over Robert's eyes, and her claws dug into his arms. She raked them through his flesh and nipped his hand with her sharp little teeth. Her *yeow* and Robert's *yeow* came out with such a deafening roar that they carried to Mrs. Rutherford and Mrs. Herbert down the hall. Robert was wiping the blood that was oozing from his arm when he saw their shocked faces.

"Robert Harrison!" exclaimed Mrs. Rutherford. "I can't believe that you would abuse a poor, defenseless animal!"

He spent the rest of the morning explaining to Mr. Yates, the counselor, Mr. Maxwell, the principal, and his parents that he was not the one at fault, but nobody seemed to believe him.

"I know how boys are," Mr. Yates said. "I'm sure you didn't *mean* to hurt Snowball, but you did. You've upset Mrs. Rutherford and you've got to realize behavior like that will not be tolerated. I've decided that you must take full responsibility for Snowball's care. Mrs. Rutherford will report your progress to me each week."

Robert spent the afternoon wishing he had killed the cat after all when he whacked it with his notebook. At least he'd have had only a punishment and not have to deal with the cat. He had to rid himself of the hideous creature, but he'd have to be very clever. He couldn't afford to make a mistake because Mrs. Rutherford, Mr. Maxwell, and Mr. Yates were watching his every move at school now.

Each night that week, Robert lay in bed reviewing all the information he'd ever picked up about cats. He didn't think of a plan until he visited his diabetic grandmother. He took the garbage out for her while she and his mom talked. As he dropped it in the dumpster, he saw a syringe sticking out. The perfect idea came in a flash. He carefully placed the syringe in his pocket.

Robert began to put his plan into action. He had read that cats loved catnip, so he began to leave a generous portion outside the storage room door each morning. Naturally Mrs. Rutherford noticed.

"How nice of you, Robert," she said. "I knew you'd like Snowball if you gave her a chance."

Robert smiled, but said nothing. It was time to put the next part of his plan into action.

In the garage, Robert had carefully mixed the rat poison. Robert filled the syringe with liquid poison, then he placed the syringe in a small plastic box that fit easily in his jacket pocket.

Scared in School

The real problem would be to get close enough to give Snowball the injection. She was still keeping a safe distance from him.

Robert knew he was still being watched. He'd have to think of some way to shift the suspicion to someone other than himself.

I wish it could be Mrs. Rutherford, he thought, and that's when his second inspiration hit him. He'd have to time it just right, but it could be done.

Robert began to monitor Mrs. Rutherford's routine as she monitored him. He observed that she left at exactly the same time every day. He noted that she parked her car in the same parking space near the old cedar tree. That was perfect! He needed the tree to carry out his plan.

Robert continued to bring catnip for Snowball. At first, she only sniffed it, but as the days passed, she began to eat it. She watched Robert closely, but when he made no attempt to hurt her, she paid less and less attention to him. Robert couldn't wait any longer. It was time to finish off Snowball forever!

He checked to see that Mrs. Rutherford's car was parked by the tree when he came to school. He fed Snowball her catnip treat and left the room with Mrs. Rutherford. When Mrs. Rutherford went in for her morning chat with Mrs. Herbert, Robert doubled back to the science room. He felt the poison-filled syringe in his jacket pocket.

He placed another supply of catnip on the floor and hid

right outside the door of the storage room. Just as he'd hoped, Snowball came out to see why she was getting a second treat. Robert's left hand shot out and grabbed Snowball while his right hand jabbed her with the needle. She struggled, but Robert held his hand over her mouth and nose until the poison took effect. He carried her into the storage room and placed her in the box where she slept. Then he tiptoed from the room. From a distance, Snowball looked as if she were sleeping peacefully. He had to take a chance that nobody would go inside the storage room and discover that she was dead.

When Robert returned for his science class before lunch, he knew all was well with his plan. He smiled at Mrs. Rutherford as he passed her desk.

"I think I'll check on Snowball before class starts," he said. "I think all that catnip is making her sleep too much."

Mrs. Rutherford followed Robert to the storage room door and looked over his shoulder.

"See what I mean?" whispered Robert.

"She looks so peaceful!" said Mrs. Rutherford. "But it might be a good idea to cut back on the catnip."

Robert was grateful that the other students were coming in now. He had counted on that. Mrs. Rutherford went back to her desk to begin class.

At lunchtime, Robert got in line with the other students so Mrs. Rutherford could escort them down to the cafeteria. He knew Mrs. Rutherford always cut out through the side door and drove down to The Teapot Restaurant to eat her own lunch.

As they turned the corner, Robert stopped at the water fountain, pretending to get a drink. Then he darted back to the room, stuffed Snowball into the bag he'd brought for this purpose, and dashed down the back stairs to Mrs. Rutherford's car. Removing the cat from the bag, he placed her under the right rear wheel and hid behind the cedar tree by Mrs. Rutherford's car and waited.

He saw her come out on schedule. She glanced at her watch and hurriedly unlocked the car door. She started the car quickly, shifted into reverse, and rolled over the cat.

Mrs. Rutherford stopped when she felt the bump and got out to investigate. When she saw what she had hit, she staggered against the car and covered her face.

Robert raced from behind the tree toward Mrs. Rutherford and the smashed cat.

"Snowball!" he called frantically.

Mrs. Rutherford looked up, thinking that Robert was coming from the cafeteria.

"Oh, Robert," she sobbed. "I've killed Snowball!"

"It wasn't your fault, Mrs. Rutherford," soothed Robert. "I'm the one to blame. I should have double-checked the door when we left the room to make sure she couldn't get out."

Mrs. Rutherford reached in her pocket and pulled out a

tissue. She began dabbing her eyes.

"You mustn't blame yourself, Robert," she said. "How could you know she'd wake up and follow us? I should have looked before I backed my car out."

By now several teachers and students had come outside to see what had happened. The sight sent most of them back inside scurrying to the restroom to lose their lunch. The custodian shook his head and got his mop from the hall storage closet.

"I'll get someone to move Snowball," Mrs. Herbert told Mrs. Rutherford. "We can't leave her here in sight during lunch."

"Please let me do it, Mrs. Rutherford," said Robert. "I have been taking care of Snowball and I'd feel better if I could do this one last thing for her."

Mrs. Rutherford began to sob again.

"Oh, Robert!" she said. "What a sweet thing to do! I knew you would learn to love Snowball. You go ahead and bury her if it will give you any comfort."

Mrs. Rutherford's body shook with more sobs as Mrs. Herbert led her away.

Robert removed his shirt and wrapped it around the cat as he lifted her from the pavement. Mrs. Rutherford looked back in time to see this and took the gesture to be a display of affection. She sobbed louder than ever as she went through the cafeteria door.

Robert carried Snowball the few blocks to his house. He

already knew where he was going to bury her. He laid her on the ground behind the garage, got his father's shovel from the tool shed, and began to dig. When he finished, he placed Snowball in a box he'd stashed in the shed and lowered it into the deep hole. He smiled as he filled in the dirt.

"That's the end of you, Snowball!" he chuckled.

As he replaced the shovel, his glee turned to uneasiness and he looked over his shoulder.

Guilty conscience, he told himself as he went to his room to replace the shirt he'd wrapped around Snowball.

He tried to shrug the feeling off as he returned to school, but it persisted even though Mrs. Rutherford gave him a hero's welcome.

Robert looked forward now to having things the way they were before Snowball had intruded in his life, but he couldn't shake the vague, uneasy feeling that was gnawing at him.

When he got home at the end of the day, his parents were waiting for him. Mrs. Rutherford had called them about Snowball's unfortunate death. They greeted Robert with mixed feelings. While they were proud that Robert had finally made peace with Snowball, they were not too happy to have a dead cat buried behind the garage.

"What's done is done," said his father, "but don't do anything like that again without asking us first."

"I won't," promised Robert.

That night in bed, Robert thought about the way fate had helped him carry out his scheme. What he did not think about was how fickle fate can be!

At midnight, a soft thud woke him. It sounded like something landing on his windowsill. He sat up in bed and listened, but not a single thing was moving in the whole house. The moonlight coming in through his window revealed nothing, but he was certain he was not alone. As he lay back down, he caught a faint whiff of catnip drifting toward his bed. He ducked under the covers and the smell vanished. It was almost morning, though, before he dared to sleep.

Kirk was not sleeping either. He was twinging with thoughts of catnip. He went to school early, knowing exactly what to do.

Robert got to class just as the bell rang. He took his seat and placed his lunch beside him as he always did. As he opened his science book, he heard a rustle from the bag. He glanced down. It seemed to have moved a few inches across the floor toward the storage room. He smelled the odor of catnip again and saw that someone had left a small pile by the door where he always put it. He began to tremble with fear and anger.

"Whoever the joker is, he's sick," Robert blurted out loudly.

Everybody turned and looked at Robert.

"What's the matter, Robert?" asked Mrs. Rutherford.

Scared in School

Robert didn't reply. He was out of his seat, heading toward the storage room. As he opened the door, a paw shot out and scratched Robert's face. He staggered forward into the room, feeling sharp little teeth nipping his neck over and over. He screamed and clutched his burning throat as a ball of white light danced in circles before his eyes and then vanished.

Mrs. Rutherford hurried to Robert and helped him to his seat. She saw Amanda Hayes watching from her seat by the door and sent her for the school nurse while she tried to calm Robert.

"What happened, Robert?" she asked over and over.

Robert was too weak now to answer. His insides burned.

Mrs. Rutherford hoped his silence meant that he was feeling better and that he had regained control of himself. Usually her students complained loudly to get attention and got quiet once everyone was looking. Still, she was relieved to see the door open and the school nurse come in.

Robert was glad to see her, too, because the pain was getting worse and he was unable to move his tongue. He could see that she was carrying something. Medicine, he hoped!

"Mrs. Rutherford," said the nurse, "will you look at this? It was right outside the door! Shall I bring it in?"

Nathan Gaylord and Kirk Radborne got up to see what the nurse was holding. Mrs. Rutherford patted Robert's shoulder and stepped closer to the nurse.

"I don't believe it!" cried Mrs. Rutherford.

Neither did Robert.

The nurse was holding an adorable little kitten almost covered in dirt! Beneath the dirt it was white, just like Snowball!

Mrs. Rutherford reached out and took the soft little kitten.

"What on earth have you dug out of?" she cooed to it. "I think you are just the thing to make Robert feel better."

Carrying the kitten, she followed the nurse toward Robert.

Take it away, please! Robert screamed in his mind. *It's come back from the grave for another life! Please don't let it near me!*

The plea never reached Robert's lips. He could only stare as he watched Mrs. Rutherford carry the kitten closer.

"Look, Robert," said Mrs. Rutherford. "It's a miniature Snowball! I think we should call it Snowflake! See how white it is under all of this dirt?"

But Robert wasn't seeing the white. He was seeing the green accusing eyes burn deep into his soul. He prayed for death, but he knew that would be too easy. He and the cat had eight more lives to go!

Belly Foot

Scrawny Nathan Gaylord collected snails, but it wasn't because he liked them. He didn't! In fact, he disliked them intensely. He liked things neat and orderly, and he was disgusted by the snails' slime. He had a good reason for tolerating it, though. He started his snail collection because his dad's new girlfriend, Miss Greta Parks, disliked them even more than he did, and he disliked her more than the snails.

He'd thought she was cool at first. Then he had not finished his math project on time. Miss Parks had kept him after school for a week until he completed it. His friends had gone without him to football practice every day. Since he didn't practice, he hadn't been able to play in the biggest game of the year!

Now Nathan's father was dating Miss Parks! The whole situation made Nathan ill every time he thought about it. He wanted to cry when he saw the two of them together. He had to find a way to break them up before they got serious. He'd die if Greta Parks became his stepmother.

Nathan had discovered Miss Parks's distaste for snails quite by accident. The night of the math fair at the PTA meeting, his father had invited Miss Parks to join them for dinner at a fancy restaurant to thank her for helping Nathan complete his project.

Nathan had not felt like celebrating. What if some of the kids from school saw them? He'd just die! He'd never hear the last of it.

"I've ordered for all of us," his father said. "It's a surprise for a special occasion."

Nathan remembered that his mother had liked it when his dad did that.

Nathan wanted his mother back home again. He wanted to sit at the dining room table and smell his mom's home-cooked meatloaf and cakes and pies. He wanted to smell her delicate lilac perfume and see her soft golden hair framing her face. She wouldn't be coming back, though. The cancer had killed her more than a year ago.

He was proud of the way she had fought the cancer to the very end. Even when the surgery and radiation didn't stop it, she didn't give up. She read about experimental drugs being used in Mexico and she had gone there to be part of the program. She had hidden some of the drugs in a false bottom in her high-heeled shoes and managed to smuggle them into the country when she came home, but, in spite of it all, the cancer had defeated her in the end.

Nathan's mother hadn't lived to finish the experimental drugs. Nathan had taken the remaining ones and had hidden them in his room in the drawer of his nightstand the day she died. His father thought he had thrown them away.

Sometimes at night, when he'd wake from a bad dream, he'd sit up and call out for his mother. Then the knowledge that she was not there would overwhelm him, and sobs would wrack his thin body. It was those times that he'd open the drawer of his nightstand and take out the bottles. Holding tightly to his mother's medication, he also clung briefly to the hope that his mother wasn't really dead. Then he'd cry until his eyes were swollen and red.

"Your mother would have been very proud of you for having the winning project at the math fair," he heard his dad saying.

Before Nathan could answer, the waiter brought the food.

Greta Parks took one look, pressed her napkin across her lips and pushed it hard to keep from gagging.

"Escargot!" she shuddered. "How can anybody eat those awful things!"

She spoke over her shoulder as she dashed for the ladies' room.

Nathan's dad signaled for the waiter to remove the orders. Nathan watched as he took them away.

Snails! thought Nathan. *Miss Parks hates snails!* He knew that information would be useful to him somehow.

"Your mother loved escargot," Nathan's dad told him. "I thought Greta would, too."

Nathan only smiled and nodded. It wasn't every day that

a guy got to see his math teacher nearly barf in a fancy restaurant.

When Miss Parks returned, she was pale but composed.

"I'm sorry for creating such a scene," she said.

The waiter returned and took their orders for steaks, baked potatoes, and salads. When the food finally came, Miss Parks only picked at her food, while Nathan and his father wolfed theirs down.

On the way home, Miss Parks kept the car window rolled down so the wind could blow in her face. Nathan managed to keep from laughing.

Nathan couldn't believe his luck the next day when Mrs. Rutherford announced in science class that they were going to begin a unit on snails.

"Today we are going to begin our study of mollusks," she said. "These are animals without backbones or bones of any kind, but usually their soft bodies are encased in shells."

"You mean like snails?" asked Nathan.

"Exactly!" said Mrs. Rutherford.

From that moment on, she had Nathan's undivided attention. As she continued her lecture, Nathan sorted out the things of interest about snails.

"A snail," she said, "has only one foot, located on its belly. Its slime gland lays a shiny pavement in front of it, so it can wriggle along at two or two-and-a-half inches a minute."

Scared in School

Miss Parks would hate those slimy trails, thought Nathan.

"A snail's tongue is called a radula," said the teacher. "It has rows of tiny, hornlike teeth. It grows continuously from the base, with rows of new teeth to replace the old ones that wear out and fall off from the front. When the snail finds something it wants to eat, it opens its big mouth and draws in the food with its tongue. The tongue works like a file to rasp off pieces of food that are then swallowed."

I could gross out Miss Parks with all of this, thought Nathan.

"Read the next chapter in your science book for your homework tonight," the teacher instructed. "Tomorrow we'll talk about where snails live and what they eat."

For once, Nathan really looked forward to his science homework. More than that, he looked forward to the evening meal. Dad had asked Miss Parks to come for dinner, and Nathan planned to talk about snails in great detail. Nathan did his homework as soon as he got home from school so he'd be ready.

As soon as they were seated at the table, Nathan put his plan into action. He barely started his vivid description of slime and snails' tongues when Miss Parks bolted from the table, gagging again. When she returned, his father ordered him to apologize and go to his room without finishing his dinner.

Hunger pangs and resentment snatched some of the joy out of Nathan's small victory. He wouldn't make the mistake of upsetting Miss Parks with talk about snails again when his dad was around, but he'd think of a way to do it at school.

The idea of collecting snails came the next day when the science teacher told the class that each of them must choose a science project. His father couldn't object to a school assignment! Nathan resolved to find a chance to expose Miss Parks to his snail project.

For the next week, Nathan read everything he could find about snails. He learned exactly where to look for them. He walked through the woods behind the house and looked under moist leaf mold. He pulled off bark from an old, rotten log and peeked inside a knothole in a large, standing tree. Back home, he looked in the damp corner of the basement. In each place, he found plump snails for his collection.

Since they were land snails, he carefully placed them in an old aquarium tank filled with soil he had prepared in advance. He brought in plants and rotting vegetation for food.

"Make sure you keep those snails in your room when Greta is here," his dad ordered. "She's coming to dinner again."

Some of the kids had learned about Miss Parks dating his dad, and they made life miserable for him with their teasing all day.

"Hey, Nathan!" Russell Newman yelled down the hall. "No wonder you got an A on your project—your dad!" He doubled over with laughter.

Scared in School

"Your momma!" Nathan yelled back.

"Not my momma, man!" shouted Russell. "She's going to be *your* momma!"

Nathan could feel the anger bubbling inside. He resented Miss Parks more than ever.

That night, Nathan was careful not to mention his snail collection during dinner. He thought he might invite his dad to look at his project after Miss Parks left, but the storm that had been threatening all evening broke as soon as she left, knocking out all the power. He and his dad went to bed early.

As Nathan dressed for school the next morning, he saw that some of his snails had died during the night. He placed them in a tissue and went out to the back yard to throw them out. A brilliant flash lit up the sky in the woods behind the school. Nathan stood watching, but he never saw another burst of light.

Nathan was turning around to go back inside when he saw it. He looked closely to be sure, but there was no mistake. It was an ear-shell snail! He couldn't imagine how it got in his back yard, but there it was! He'd read about it in one of the science books he'd checked out from the public library. He found it especially fascinating because, unlike most snails, it was a flesh eater! It lived underground, feeding on earthworms and other snails and coming out only at night or after a soaking rain like the one last night.

"You will be the star of my collection at the science fair," said Nathan, as he picked it up. "I'm going to call you Belly Foot."

Nathan hurried to his room and placed his newest prize in the tank where the dead snails had been. He went outside again and found some earthworms for Belly Foot to eat. He moistened the soil the best he could.

When he got home that afternoon, he found Belly Foot on the surface of the soil looking all dried out.

Nathan had no idea what to do. What kind of medicine did a sick snail need? He would ask Mrs. Rutherford first thing tomorrow.

He sat cross-legged on the floor and stared at the snail for several minutes. It didn't move at all. He thought of calling Mrs. Rutherford at home, but he doubted she'd be there yet. He poked the snail with his finger, but there was no response. If it wasn't dead already, it was certainly close!

Then he remembered the experimental drugs his mother had taken before she died. Maybe they would help. He had to try something because his project was due at school in the morning.

Nathan opened the drawer of his nightstand and took out the bottles. His mother had warned him that he must never take any of her medication, but surely it wouldn't hurt a snail! He opened the first bottle and dropped one drop of the dark red liquid on the snail. Then he repeated the process with the dirty brown liquid in the second bottle. After about ten seconds, the snail jerked and began to move around.

He decided he'd better take the medication to school with him in case the snail got sick again. He figured it would be easier to carry to school if he mixed the contents of both bottles together. He poured a generous amount over the dirt before he left his room.

Nathan thought little about the snail throughout dinner. He watched TV for an hour with his father and then went up to do his homework. He was sitting at his desk working on the math problems Miss Parks had given the class. A loud thump in the tank brought his attention back to the snail. As Nathan stared at it, the thump came again and the tank slid several inches on the table. Nathan stood up, backed against the door just as the dirt broke open and the snail emerged from where it had burrowed. Nathan groped for the doorknob and held on tightly, his eyes widening in terror. The snail was four times bigger than it was when he left.

It opened its mouth and Nathan could see its tongue covered with rows of teeth. It was probably hungry, but he had nothing in the room to feed it but the medication. He knew he should not give it more, but he had to do something. Until he could figure out what to do with it, he couldn't let it keep moving around, thumping the tank.

Nathan slowly circled the room toward the nightstand,

leaving as much room as possible between himself and the tank. He found the bottle in the nightstand drawer and poured the rest of the medication into the tank. The snail jerked several times and became calmer.

Nathan tried to fall asleep, but he couldn't. He kept thinking about how fast the snail had grown. He got up and eased himself to the tank for another look. The snail was looking at him!

Just as he began to back away from the tank, Nathan heard the phone ringing. Nathan stood paralyzed and watched the snail burrow back beneath the soil in the tank. Then his father called him. Nathan left the snail and went downstairs.

"That was a call from my boss," his father told him. "I have to go in early in the morning, so I can't drive you to school with your science project. I'm going to call Greta to come by and pick you up."

"But, Dad," Nathan reminded him, "my project is snails. You know how Miss Parks hates snails."

"Just ride in the back seat and keep the tank covered so she won't see them."

"But, Dad, there's a problem," Nathan began.

"Can't it wait, son?" said his dad, cutting him off. "I've got to get to sleep if I'm going in early."

"Sure, Dad," said Nathan.

Nathan followed his father up the stairs. The snail was at

rest, and he began to relax. He'd have to try to get the snail to school so he could ask Mrs. Rutherford about it. It might even be funny if Miss Parks did get a glimpse of Belly Foot! He could just imagine her reaction.

Nathan fell asleep quickly this time. During the night, he heard a loud thump from the tank. He had nothing to feed the snail, so he didn't get up. He wished he'd never given it that medication!

Nathan woke the next morning to the sound of voices in the kitchen. Miss Parks had come early to have breakfast with his dad, no doubt. Nathan dressed quickly. He would have to get the snail down to the car before it woke up hungry again.

As he crossed to the door, he noticed it was open. His father must have looked in on him before he went downstairs. In the hall light, he noticed something glistening on the floor. He looked closer and saw the wide, shiny trail of slime leading from his room to the hall bathroom. He whirled and looked at the tank across the room. He was shocked to see it was overturned and the dirt spilled on the floor.

Nathan grabbed a dirty shirt from a chair by his bed and wiped up as much of the slime as he could while he worked his way to the bathroom. The door was partially open and he could see that something was inside. He inched up as close as he dared and took a closer look. His heart nearly stopped. He couldn't believe he was seeing such a gruesome monster, yet he knew he was not imagining it.

The snail had grown until it now filled the bathroom. Its mouth was open, exposing rows and rows of teeth.

Nathan knew he had to keep it inside until he could tell his father and get help. He opened the hall closet door quietly, taking care not to attract the snail's attention. He removed a coat hanger from the closet, hooked it over the knob, and yanked the bathroom door shut. Nathan stood there trembling. The door had clicked shut just as the huge, searching tongue had rasped against it.

Nathan's knees buckled and he sank to the hall floor. He had to tell his dad before he left, but he found it difficult to get up. He forced himself to stand, but his steps were wobbly as he moved toward the stairs. He was turning blind and he knew he was going to be sick.

"Dad!" he called, flinging his arms out for something to hold onto. The stairs melted into the darkness that engulfed him as he crumpled to the floor.

Slowly Nathan came out of the blackness. His dad and Miss Parks were kneeling beside him.

"He's never fainted before," he heard his dad say.

"I'll get a cold washcloth," he heard Miss Parks say, and he saw her stand and start toward the bathroom.

"No!" he tried to say, but the sound wouldn't come out.

"Take it easy, son" said his dad. "You're going to be fine."

Scared in School

Nathan rolled his head from side to side as the most unearthly shriek he'd ever heard came from the bathroom.

"No, Dad, stop!" Nathan managed to say, but the warning went unheard.

From his place on the floor, Nathan saw his father stop for one split second at the door. His one scream of mortal terror was cut halfway off when Belly Foot's tongue shot out and encircled him.

Nathan tried to get up, but he was too dizzy to stand. He sat sobbing while everything whirled around him, until the moment Belly Foot followed a trail of slime down the hall, hungry for dessert.

Hall Walker

Nothing was strange at first about Addie Forest's daily walk at 13th Street Middle School. She had decided to make walking a part of her daily physical fitness program, so every morning at nine-thirty, she took a break from her library duties and walked through the second floor hallway. She had to walk around the second floor seven times to complete a mile. Addie usually walked five miles a day.

Addie was a kind lady who always smiled at anyone she met along the way, even the custodian who looked annoyed when she walked on his freshly mopped floor. Some people, just a little envious of her progress, teased her occasionally, but it was all good-natured fun and Addie Forest took it in that spirit. She was determined that nothing was going to keep her from walking.

One person who teased Addie was Mrs. Tanner, whose language arts classroom was near the end of the hall.

"I can set my clock by you, Addie," Mrs. Tanner called as Addie passed her doorway for the fourth time one morning. "I guess you are going to walk these halls forever!"

"I guess I will!" Addie called back without missing a stride.

Mrs. Tanner smiled as her friend walked by. She truly

admired Addie and she knew that Addie understood that in spite of the teasing. Mrs. Tanner turned back to her class and thought no more about Addie that day.

Mrs. Tanner's second period class was her worst group of the day. If she turned her back, they threw spitballs. If she gave a writing assignment, they wrote more dirty words on their desks than clean words on their papers. Some insisted on writing with pencils instead of pens so they could deliberately break off the points and disrupt the class by going to the pencil sharpener. Lately, two of her more disruptive students had begun to come to class late every day.

"There's no excuse for them to be out walking the halls every day," Mrs. Tanner complained to Mr. Maxwell.

"Mrs. Tanner, the boys tell me they have been getting out of P.E. late," explained Mr. Maxwell. "I'm checking into it."

"They told me that, too," said Mrs. Tanner, "but I've talked to the teacher and the other students and they all tell me that the class ends on time. If the other students can avoid being tardy, I'm sure Tyrone Hale and Jerry Madden can do it, too."

"I'll talk to them again and see what I can do," promised Mr. Maxwell, dismissing Mrs. Tanner with a nod of his head.

"Humph!" Mrs. Tanner muttered. She had heard that promise before when the same two boys threatened to beat her up last semester. Nothing had ever been done except the two boys had been removed from her class for a few weeks and made office aides. The time out of class and the extra freedom to roam the halls on errands with an office hall pass did not seem like much of a punishment to her.

The boys received nothing this time but a verbal reprimand. Tyrone and Jerry continued to roam around after the tardy bell, and Mrs. Tanner continued to write referrals that were ignored.

One day Mrs. Tanner had looked out the window and seen them in the faculty parking lot. That afternoon when she started home, she discovered that her tires had been slashed. Tyrone and Jerry swore that they knew nothing about it and the matter was dropped. After that, Mrs. Tanner left her car at home and had her husband drop her off at school. Tyrone and Jerry made several snide remarks about bad boys picking on little old ladies, but she pretended she didn't hear. She could do nothing without proof, and she apparently had none that would impress Mr. Maxwell.

After getting away with that escapade, the boys grew more confident that they could do whatever they wanted to do and get away with it. The two boys began walking the halls between most of their classes, threatening other students, and vandalizing lockers, restrooms, and water fountains. There never seemed to be any witnesses to their antics; the truth was, everybody was afraid to admit they had seen anything for fear of being the next victim.

Scared in School

Addie Forest was the exception. She happened to be out in the hall one morning on her daily walk when she saw the two boys grab a girl's purse and shove her against the wall. Addie hurried to the girl and helped her up. Then she went straight to Mr. Maxwell and reported the incident.

The next morning, both boys were back in school. Mr. Maxwell made a point of telling Addie that the purse had been returned and that he had cleared everything up with a telephone conference with the parents.

Addie was still upset about the incident when she passed Mrs. Tanner's room on her morning walk.

"Those boys were really angry with me because I reported them," said Addie. "I got a threatening phone call last night and I am sure it was one of them. It will take something awful, I suppose, before anything is done about those two."

"You're probably right," Mrs. Tanner agreed. "Just be careful."

As Addie Forest walked on down the hall, Mrs. Tanner noticed her steps were slow and heavy. The custodian grimly mopped at her heels.

It's a shame that someone as nice as Addie is treated that way, Mrs. Tanner thought to herself.

She watched until Addie turned the corner and then she turned to go into her own classroom. She had just stepped inside the door when she heard the scream.

"Oh, my Lord, it's Addie!" she gasped.

Mrs. Tanner hit the emergency button in her room to summon help. She ran down the hall and turned the corner. Her students, except for Tyrone and Jerry, were right behind her.

The halls were full of other teachers and students now, pouring out of nearby classrooms. Mrs. Tanner pushed through the crowd at the top of the stairs. At the bottom of the stairwell lay Addie Forest, the side of her head bashed in and bleeding. The twisted angle of her neck left no doubt that she was dead.

Mrs. Tanner turned and ran, blinded by tears. She bumped into someone at the front edge of the crowd. She wiped her eyes and saw that it was Tyrone Hale talking under his breath to Jerry Madden!

"... got what she deserved!" Mrs. Tanner heard him say. Jerry Madden was smiling and nodding his head in agreement.

At that moment, Mrs. Tanner would have rejoiced if someone had sent both boys to the same fate as Addie's.

Rumors circulated that Tyrone and Jerry had been seen pushing Addie Forest down the stairs. Even though nobody was willing to go to the police, the rumors were strong enough to scare Tyrone and Jerry into coming to class on time the day of Addie's funeral. Their presence was a hateful thing to Mrs. Tanner now. She believed with all her heart that because of them, Addie was gone.

The halls will be empty now, thought Mrs. Tanner.

Scared in School

Mrs. Tanner spent the weekend after Addie Forest's funeral in a daze. She arrived at school early Monday morning and went to her room to try to grade papers, though she had trouble concentrating. At nine o'clock, her class came in, subdued for once. Tyrone and Jerry were on time, but Mrs. Tanner could see that they had slipped some filthy magazines inside their books and were pretending to read the lesson. She ignored them. She knew that she could do nothing to salvage those two anyway. Sometimes a teacher had to admit that she couldn't reach every single student. She had failed with these boys, so it was better to save her energy for the students who really wanted to learn.

Mrs. Tanner moved her chair near the door and continued to grade papers while the students read. She tried not to think about Addie, but she couldn't help it. At nine-thirty A.M., a movement in the hall caught her eye. She looked up and saw Addie Forest gliding down the hall! Addie looked as alive and as real as she ever did, except for the head wound and the twisted neck. Mrs. Tanner was too shocked to move or make a sound.

Seeing that Mrs. Tanner was distracted, although he didn't know why, Tyrone Hale seized the opportunity to announce that he had to go to the restroom. Mrs. Tanner made a half-hearted move to stop him, even though he took the hall pass without permission. It wasn't that Tyrone felt he needed a pass. He just wanted to bug Mrs. Tanner by taking something from her desk.

He'd barely had time to reach the corner near the stairway when Mrs. Tanner heard him scream. It wasn't the deep whoop she often heard him make when bullying other students in the hallway, but a high-pitched shriek. Mrs. Tanner managed to get up and reach the hall in time to see Tyrone Hale running for his life! Behind him, she could see the ghostly form of Addie Forest floating right along.

Mrs. Tanner was beyond terror now. She watched, feeling nothing at all. It was like watching an old, silent movie, except there was nothing silent about the screams tearing from Tyrone's throat. At first everybody thought Tyrone was playing some kind of joke, but they knew the screams were too real for that. Heads popped out of doorways as the boy raced down the hall. Several of Mrs. Tanner's students came to the door and looked over her shoulder to see what was happening.

Mrs. Tanner thought Tyrone would turn when he reached the other end of the hall, but he didn't! She heard a shattering of glass in the hall window, one long scream before the thud, and then silence.

The witnesses stood unable to believe their own eyes. Then a babble of voices erupted.

"What happened?"

"I'm not sure!"

"Did you see him?"

Scared in School

"Craziest thing I ever saw!"

"Quick! Somebody get some help down here!"

Mrs. Tanner saw her hall pass on the floor where Tyrone had dropped it. She quietly picked it up.

People were still milling around in the hall asking questions.

They don't know what really happened! she thought. *I am the only one who saw Addie chase Tyrone through that window!*

"I always knew one of Tyrone's practical jokes would do him in," Mrs. Tanner heard a voice behind her say. She turned to see Mr. McClure, the social studies teacher, standing near his room.

Mrs. Tanner didn't contradict him. In a way, he was right. It had started out as one of Tyrone's jokes. It would be better to let everyone think that the joke had turned into a tragic accident. She certainly wasn't going to mention that Addie Forest's ghost was walking the halls now if no one else was aware of it!

Tyrone's funeral was on Wednesday. Mrs. Tanner didn't go. She offered to keep some of the other teachers' classes so they could attend, but none of them seemed to want to go any more than she did. She heard later that even Jerry Madden had run out when the service began.

Jerry was absent from school on Thursday and Friday. On Monday morning, he swaggered into Mrs. Tanner's class as if nothing had happened. It was evident that he had come to disrupt. He refused to take his seat for five minutes. He talked when Mrs. Tanner was talking. He dropped his book on the floor with a bang and laughed when everyone jumped. At first, Mrs. Tanner ignored him. That had no effect at all. Then she reprimanded him. That only made him worse. He began to hum and whistle. Mrs. Tanner knew there was no need to write a referral to the office, but an idea came to her. She looked at the clock and made a decision. It was nearly nine-thirty. She would tolerate Jerry a few minutes longer.

She gave the class a reading assignment and moved her chair over by the door. At half-past-nine, she glanced out the door and saw what she was looking for. The time had come for her to put her plan into action. She had a challenge for Jerry Madden that he couldn't refuse.

Jerry had continued to disrupt all this time just as she knew he would. First, he broke apart a ballpoint pen and smeared ink on the desktop. He folded a small piece of paper, stuffed it in the now empty cylinder of the pen, and blew it across the aisle. He eyed Mrs. Tanner to see if she'd noticed.

"If you don't behave, you'll be sorry, Jerry," warned Mrs. Tanner.

"And what will you do about it if I don't, you ugly old woman?" sneered Jerry.

"I am going to sit right here to make sure you stay in this class today, young man," she told him.

Scared in School

"Oh, yeah?" he said.

Mrs. Tanner knew he couldn't resist defying her. She knew exactly what he'd do, and he did not disappoint her.

Jerry Madden got up and strolled to her desk. He picked up her hall pass and headed toward the door, waving the pass so everyone could see that he was taking it without her permission. He paused by Mrs. Tanner's chair.

"I think I've got a little business at my locker," he told her. "Don't get in my way, old lady!"

Mrs. Tanner pretended to be shocked when Jerry walked by her. She stood up quickly and locked the door behind him. She looked at the clock and smiled. She had timed it just right. It was nine-thirty on the dot when she started her plan. Addie Forest was coming down the hall grinning, and Jerry Madden was taking his last walk!

Shoe Souls

Step, drag! Step, drag!

Hobert Burton watched Josh Morgan move across the 13th Street Middle School playground, dragging his heavily braced leg as he inched his way toward the baseball field.

Surely he doesn't expect anyone to pick him for their team! thought Hobert.

Step, drag! Step, drag!

Josh hadn't played baseball since last New Year's Eve, when the school bus he was riding was forced off the road by a drunk driver. He would have been the star player this year, but the accident had ended that. The crash had splintered a tree—and Josh's leg—and he knew as soon as it happened that neither would grow straight again.

Step, drag! Step, drag!

Josh was leaning against the fence behind home plate, probably to take pressure off the leg for a minute. Hobert saw that Josh was staring at him again. He hated it when Josh did that!

"Hey, Crip!" yelled Hobert. "What are you looking at?"

Josh held his gaze steady and didn't answer.

"Get lost, Creep!" Hobert yelled again.

Scared in School

"That'll be enough, Burton!" called Coach Richards. "Get on the field!"

"But, Coach!" Hobert protested. "He stares at me all the time! Tell him to lay off! My brother was drunk—not me! I didn't hit that school bus!"

"Try to see it the way he does," said Coach Richards. "He used to get chosen first for every game. Now he's got a crippled leg, your brother's got probation, and you've got his spot on the baseball team! Give him a break! OK?"

"OK," Hobert muttered, but it made him angry that the coach always got on him instead of Josh. Just once, he'd like to see the coach tell Josh Morgan to take a hike!

"You're catching, Burton," said the coach. "Get with it!"

Hobert walked over by the fence where Josh was still leaning. He glanced at the coach to see if he was watching. He was! Hobert turned away from Josh to assume his position behind David Palmer, who was at bat, but he couldn't help noticing Josh's new designer shoes. He looked down at his own shoes that his mother bought at the discount shoe store at the mall. He wished he had an uncle who owned a shoe store, like Josh did.

I could fly if I had Josh's shoes, he thought. *It's not fair. He doesn't need shoes like that. He doesn't even appreciate them. He's already got the right one dirty from dragging it through the dust.*

Step, drag! Step, drag!

At the sound, Hobert turned to see Josh moving from

behind the fence to the bleachers along the side of the field. Hobert couldn't take his eyes off the new shoes until he heard the coach's voice loud and angry. Hobert's attention focused back on the game, but it was too late. David Palmer had hit a foul ball and Hobert had failed to catch it!

Hobert heard Josh's laugh over the coach's voice, but he dared not turn away from the coach to look over in Josh's direction.

Step, drag! Step, drag!

Josh left the bleachers and made his way slowly back to the school building. He was out of sight by the time Hobert was up to bat. Hobert swung and hit the ball high over center field, but it was a hollow victory since Josh hadn't seen it.

When the game was over, Hobert showered and headed home. As he walked down the steps, he saw Laura Kirk standing by the curb. He'd waited all week to catch her alone to ask her to the spring dance. He hadn't had the courage to ask her with her friends around. This would be a perfect chance!

Step, drag! Step, drag!

Hobert couldn't believe what he was hearing! Josh Morgan couldn't be showing up now. Hobert didn't look back. He hurried straight to Laura.

"Hi, Laura," he said. "Could I walk you home? I've got something I want to ask you."

"Thanks," said Laura, "but I've got plans for today!"

Scared in School

Step, drag! Step, drag!

The new designer shoes were now standing next to Hobert's old, shabby ones.

"Hi, Josh," said Laura. "I'm ready!"

Hobert looked from one to the other.

"Josh is taking me shopping for shoes at his uncle's store," explained Laura. "I need some for cheerleading and he can get me a great buy."

"Oh," said Hobert.

"Want to come with us?" asked Josh. "I can get you a good deal, too."

"No, thanks," Hobert said coldly, determined not to let Laura see how upset he was. "I've got to get home."

Hobert felt his face getting hot as he turned and walked away.

"What did you want to ask me?" called Laura.

"Nothing," answered Hobert, and he hurried on without looking back.

Hobert was quiet all during dinner, but inside he was seething. He didn't see why everybody felt so sorry for Josh Morgan! He got all the attention and now he had Laura Kirk, too! Life wasn't fair. It always threw you a curve just when you thought you'd won the game.

Hobert helped his mom clear the table in order to get his mind off Josh and Laura. Maybe they were just going shopping for shoes. Maybe Josh hadn't meant anything by saying he could get Hobert a deal, but Hobert didn't think so! He was sure he was making fun of his shoes. The more he thought of it, the more he wanted to teach Josh a lesson.

"I need to go to the library for a while," Hobert called to his mom.

He hurried out of the house before his mom could object. He had to get some air. He turned down the street in the direction of the library in case his mom was watching out the window.

He had walked a couple of blocks when he realized that Laura's house was around the next corner. If he walked by, he might run into her and get another chance to ask her to the dance. It was certainly worth a try.

As he turned the corner, he could see her front porch clearly. She was there alright, just has he'd hoped, but someone was with her. He stayed in the shadows until he was close enough to see that it was Josh! Hobert stood staring as Laura leaned forward and kissed Josh before going inside.

Step, drag! Step, drag!

Josh was walking up the street in his direction. Hobert ducked between two cars parked at the curb. Josh approached and started to cross the street. At that moment, a car swerved around the corner and careened toward the sidewalk. Josh saw it coming and tried to run. Before he could move, Hobert's hands shot out from between the two cars and shoved Josh forward into the path of the oncoming car. The metal brace clanged against the bumper as the car screeched to a halt. Then there was silence.

Hobert sat too shocked to move. He hadn't meant to shove Josh, but he had been unable to resist the urge. People were rushing into the street now, and Hobert slipped into the shadows and disappeared around the corner.

Then he ran. When he was in front of the library, he stopped. He would have to get a book to prove where he'd been in case his mother was still up. A few minutes later, he came out of the library, book in hand, and walked home. Hobert heard his mother and his brother, Keith, talking when he came down for breakfast the next morning.

"It's that same kid, Mom," Keith was saying. "The paper says the boy's feet were cut right off in his shoes when the car hit him. They had to search for half an hour before they found them. It was just like they walked off all by themselves."

"What are you talking about?" asked Hobert. He had intended to act surprised when he heard about the accident, but his surprise was genuine when he heard about Josh's feet.

"That boy Josh Morgan was killed last night," said Hobert's mom. "The driver had a heart attack and lost control of the car. It was right before you came home from the library. Didn't you hear the sirens?"

"Yes," said Hobert, "but I didn't really think much about

it. I hear sirens every time I go out."

"I'm glad you didn't go over there," said his mom. "It would have looked bad since your brother was the cause of that first accident."

Keith sighed and left the room. Hobert left shortly after.

Josh Morgan's death was the subject on everybody's mind at school that day. When Hobert saw Laura after school, she seemed to be glad that he fell into step with her and walked her home. She was pleased to have company for support.

Hobert made a point of being extra kind and concerned. He was careful not to say the slightest thing against Josh. There was no way anyone could connect him with the death of Josh Morgan. He was in no danger if he just kept calm and played the waiting game!

Hobert *was* calm when he went to bed that night. He was just dozing off when he heard it.

Step, drag! Step, drag!

Hobert sat up in bed and listened. He was sure he had been dreaming. He hoped he had been dreaming! He had heard Josh's footsteps distinctly. He forced himself to lie down again and go back to sleep. He woke the next morning when he heard his mom cry out. He hurried downstairs and saw his mom and brother staring out the front door.

"What is it?" asked Hobert.

"Footprints!" said his mom. "I went to get the paper and

there they were! Bloody footprints leading to the door!"

"It's probably one of those nutty organizations that hasn't forgotten that I was in that accident," said his brother. "Go on in. I'll clean these off the porch."

Hobert glanced at the footprints as his brother closed the door. Actually, it was one footprint and one smeared line, another clear print, another smeared line. *Step, drag!* There was no doubt that they belonged to Josh! That was impossible, though. He was dead!

But who could have done it? Who else knew? Hobert was very much afraid of the answers to his questions.

All day at school, Hobert heard the sound. *Step, drag! Step, drag!* He looked over his shoulder a dozen times, but it was only in his mind. Nobody else heard!

Hobert dreaded bedtime. He was afraid of the dreams. For that matter, he was afraid of reality. He carefully placed his baseball bat beside his bed before he went to sleep.

Step, drag! Step, drag!

Hobert was wide awake, listening.

Step, drag! Step, drag!

Someone or something was inside the house now, coming up the steps!

Step, drag! Step, drag!

It stopped outside Hobert's door. He clutched his heart to make it be still, but it pounded in terror!

Roberta Simpson Brown

The door was opening slowly. Hobert tried to call out for his mom and brother, but he couldn't speak. It came at him with the fury of hell!

Step drag step drag step drag step drag!

Swiftly, violently, it was over!

When Hobert's mother entered his bedroom to wake him in the morning, an eerie silence greeted her. Hobert lay with his dead eyes fixed toward the ceiling. Across his chest was his splintered baseball bat, and beside his bed was a pair of bloody designer sneakers.

Cutting

Warm, stale air rushed at Kevin Hale as he opened the storage room door and quickly closed it behind him. He was amazed that the door had been unlocked. When he had decided to cut his science class, he was sure he would have to hide out in the restroom. Things were looking up at 13th Street Middle School!

He didn't know why he had tried this particular door. As he'd walked by, he'd felt a strong urge to open it and he'd acted on the impulse. Now he was glad he did. His chances of being caught cutting class were much slimmer in here than in the restroom.

He groped along the wall for the light switch. His fingers touched it and flipped it on. Gradually, objects emerged from the shadows in the light of the dim bulb—indistinct at first, then clearly. As his eyes adjusted, he noted there was enough light to see by if he wanted to read his comic books later. Right now he was interested only in exploring his new hideout.

He could see that the room had obviously not been used for some time. Cobwebs hung from the top shelves and the faint odor of chemicals clung to empty test tubes and bottles stored in open boxes. In one cardboard box, Kevin found scissors, knives of various sizes, and a few other discarded instruments he'd never bothered to learn about.

A large carton on the floor was filled with outdated science books. Kevin dusted off the top and sat down to decide what to do next. He looked at his bookbag that held the new comic books he'd traded his baseball cards for, and he looked at the brown paper bag which held his lunch. He opened the brown paper bag first. He'd eat some now and the rest later in the cafeteria with his pals.

He took out a ham and cheese sandwich and began to munch it as he flopped open a comic book across his knees. For some reason, the words did not register in his mind this morning. His thoughts were wandering back to his old school.

He had been doing so well there until they began to study frogs. Old Mrs. Hall was an animal rights activist, and she had told the class they would not do any dissecting! That had really annoyed Kevin. That was the one thing he'd looked forward to. He had decided to get even with her if he could find a way, and he couldn't believe how she had freaked out when the opportunity for revenge presented itself.

Kevin let his mind drift back to the day he'd been suspended permanently from North Lake School. He'd cut class that day because Mrs. Hall's lectures were so boring. There was no point in going to lab if they weren't going to dissect frogs. He liked cutting animals! He'd done it secretly for years in the woods behind his former home.

First it had been a mouse that he'd caught and removed from the house while his mother stood on a chair and shrieked. He'd meant to bury it in the woods, but he had been seized by curiosity as to what it was like inside.

Next, it was his neighbor's cat. The old woman had yelled at him for chasing her cat through her flower beds. Then she'd snatched up the cat and hurried inside muttering that cats were much better than children. That night, he'd caught the cat outside and taken it to the woods. The old woman looked at him accusingly whenever she saw him outside after that, but he knew she couldn't prove a thing.

He had made other plans and carried them out—some more successfully than others—but he really wasn't planning any mischief the day he got suspended.

He'd gone outside that day to avoid being caught cutting, and he was sneaking toward the cafeteria at noon to join his friends at lunch. When he walked by the science room on the way, he noticed that the window was open. Some frogs that two boys had brought for a special project were croaking in Mrs. Hall's holding tank by the window. He looked in and saw that the room was empty, except for the frogs. He eased himself through the window and turned to the tank. It didn't take long to do what he wanted to do.

He found a long, sharp knife in one of the cabinets. One

by one, he lifted the frogs from the tank and thrust the knife deep into their throats. There in the storage room, he could still picture them clearly in his mind as they jumped and croaked that day. He hadn't been distracted. He'd kept cutting and cutting. When he'd finished, he'd arranged them on the lab table in the outline of a boy.

He had just finished when Mrs. Hall returned from lunch. She looked at him and she looked at the table of mutilated frogs, and then her lunch came up all over the floor.

Kevin had thought it was funny until her shrieks brought the principal and teachers running from nearby rooms. They hadn't seen the humor in it at all, and neither had his parents when they arrived at school later to learn their son would have to leave North Lake School for good!

Kevin's counselor had suggested a private school where Kevin could get more attention, but the family budget couldn't support that. His mom and dad both had to work as it was, just to make ends meet. The board of education finally granted Kevin a hardship transfer to 13th Street Middle School, which was near his mother's work place so she could drop him off and pick him up every day.

He had tried at first to attend all his classes and do well here. He wore his black and red uniform every day and did his homework every night, but it had been hard. News of his escapades at North Lake had reached 13th Street School, and all the good kids avoided him. His only friends were a pair of trou-blemakers who seemed to admire what he'd done. Then this morning, the counselor, Mr. Yates, had told Kevin that his sched-ule had been changed so he wouldn't see his pals except at lunch. That was the last straw. That's why he'd decided to skip class today. It would be boring without his buddies. He was thrilled that he'd found the storage room so quickly. He'd tell his friends about it at lunch and maybe persuade them to come back here with him instead of going to math.

Kevin glanced around the room to see if anything might be of special interest to the other boys. The light seemed dimmer now than when he first came in. Objects seemed to take on dif-ferent shapes in the far corners. Kevin began to feel uneasy now.

"Get a grip, man," he muttered to himself. "Your mind's playing tricks."

Kevin turned his complete attention to his comic book. He was able to lose himself in the story this time. When he fin-ished the first book, he put it back into his bag and took out another one. He smiled as he opened it across his knees.

Fate must have helped me find this place, he thought.

As he rustled the first page of his comic book, he heard a faint rustling in the corner. For an instant, Kevin had the strangest feeling that someone was watching him.

That's silly, he told himself, but he glanced around any-way.

Nothing was there, so he looked back at the book. This time, a low creak interrupted his reading. Looking up, he saw a cabinet door partially open. He was sure it had been closed when he first came in.

Must be warped or something, he thought.

He started to read again, but a movement inside the cabinet caught his attention.

"Maybe it's a mouse," he said to himself.

Something inside him knew it wasn't a mouse. He had to know what it was.

He stood up and moved toward the cabinet. Suddenly, a loud hiss came from behind him. Something unseen brushed against his leg and was gone before he could move. At the same time, Kevin heard a low laugh. He whirled around and saw a boy standing in the shadows by the old tank on the cabinet.

"Gotcha!" said the boy.

"OK, so you scared me," said Kevin. "Big deal! What are you really doing here?" As his eyes adjusted, he noticed that while the boy was wearing a school uniform, the slacks and shirt were green instead of the normal black and red.

"I came here to cut, like you," the boy answered.

Kevin had been more frightened by the intruder than he cared to admit, but he began to relax now.

"I found this place, but you can stay if you like," said Kevin. "Would you like to read one of my comics?"

Scared in School

The boy ignored the question.

"I know what you did at North Lake," he said, moving a step closer to Kevin.

"So what?" said Kevin, beginning to feel uneasy again.

The boy stepped from the shadows and stood in front of Kevin.

"So this!" sneered the boy. Kevin was shocked to see a webbed hand grab at him.

Kevin staggered back. His heart began to pound so hard he thought it was breaking out of his chest. This couldn't be real! He had to be dreaming, but he knew he wasn't.

"Get away!" he screamed, but his voice came out in a hoarse croak. "Get away from me!"

Kevin reached for the doorknob behind him and gave it a hard turn. The door wouldn't open.

The figure from the shadows moved closer to Kevin. It was changing now. The green uniform now had raised green splotches that were turning into rough, stretched green skin. The bulging eyes were fixed on Kevin's face. Even in the dim light, Kevin could see that the thing held something shiny. He knew what it was. Kevin's knees buckled under him as the thing approached. Then it thrust the knife deep into Kevin's throat and kept cutting and cutting and cutting!

Erasers

Kenny Phillips stuffed his books into his locker and slammed the door. He watched his best buddy Rick walk toward the bus exit at 13th Street Elementary School. Then Kenny headed down the hall to Miss Payne's room for detention. Only Miss Payne would hold detention the last week of school.

She's got the right name, thought Kenny. *She's a pain all right!*

He didn't deserve detention today. All he'd done was blow some chalk dust on Kay Durham when she wouldn't let him read her note. The way Miss Payne reacted, you'd have thought it was radioactive fallout!

"You will stay after school for one hour," she ordered, "and you will clean the chalkboard and erasers!"

He thought about telling her he was allergic to chalk dust, but decided against it. Knowing her, he figured she'd probably haul him off to the doctor to check out his story!

He paused outside the door, dreading to go in. He hated working by himself while she sat behind her desk watching his every move.

Then for a second, he took heart! A shadow passed over the glass panes in the door. Maybe he'd have company today!

Maybe she'd kept some other poor kid!

He opened the door and stepped inside, and immediately his spirits fell. Miss Payne was sitting behind her desk, and a quick scan of the room told Kenny nobody else was there.

"You are one minute late, Kenny," said Miss Payne, standing up to rummage through her briefcase. "Please get started at once."

Kenny had no more time to think about the shadow. He picked up an eraser and began to erase the board. The dust particles floated around the eraser and tickled Kenny's nose. It had an odd, sweet smell today, like Candace Golding's hair when she sat in front of him in class yesterday. It couldn't be her, though. She was absent today.

"This chalk dust smells funny," he said aloud.

"Yes," agreed Miss Payne. "That's my fault. I'm afraid I made a mistake in choosing it."

Kenny stopped with the eraser in his hand. He couldn't believe that he had actually heard Miss Payne say she had made a mistake. The dust particles tickled his nose again and he sneezed. The shadow passed over his face again, black like the board, and, for a second, the surface of the board shimmered before his eyes. He blinked and everything was normal.

He heard Miss Payne mumble something inaudible as she snapped the lock on her briefcase.

"Did you say something to me, Miss Payne?" asked

Kenny.

She looked displeased that he had heard her.

"Bless you," she said. "When you sneezed, that's all I said."

Kenny didn't think so. It sounded more like a scolding than a blessing. But why would she be scolding her briefcase?

Maybe we are both going crazy, thought Kenny.

He turned back to his chore, hurrying so that he could leave. As he rubbed the wet sponge across the board, he heard a soft moan. He'd made the board screech before, but it had never sounded like this.

When he began to beat the erasers to remove the excessive dust, Miss Payne stood up.

"I don't like to smell the dust," she told Kenny. "You continue, but I am going to wait outside until you finish."

She leaned over and snapped open the lock on her briefcase before she left.

That's weird, thought Kenny. *Why would she unlock it?* Unless, of course, this was some kind of test. That must be it! She wanted to catch Kenny looking in her briefcase so she could detain him again! *Well, sorry, lady!* he thought. *It won't work!*

Kenny finished before his hour was up and started to the door to call Miss Payne. Before he reached it, the door opened and Miss Payne came back inside.

Her face looked tense and white.

Scared in School

"You disappoint me, Kenny," she said.

"How?" asked Kenny, though he assumed she was referring to the fact that he hadn't opened the briefcase. He acted as if he hadn't noticed the trap she'd set for him. "I finished early."

"I dislike having to take a personal hand in these matters," she said, "but sometimes you unruly students leave me no choice."

"But I did what you told me," Kenny pointed out. "See how clean the board is? There's not a speck of chalk on it."

"True," she said. "It will be hungry now."

"What?" asked Kenny. He was beginning to feel frightened. He wished she wasn't standing between him and the door. He had been right! She was crazy! He wondered if he should try to make a run for it.

"Don't try to get away, Kenny," she warned. She obviously read his thoughts. "It will only make things harder for you."

"I don't know what you're talking about," said Kenny, taking a couple of steps back toward the chalkboard.

"I know you don't, Kenny," she smiled. "All of you troublemakers are the same. You never listen. I tell you to behave and you ignore me."

She took a step forward, and Kenny looked quickly at the window. He knew he could never escape that way, though. They were on the second floor. Maybe he could reason with her until he could figure out what to do.

"I'm sorry, Miss Payne," he said. "I only blew chalk dust at Kay."

Miss Payne moved closer. Her eyes were narrow slits now, set on him.

"You disturbed the others," she said.

"I didn't disturb anybody but Kay," said Kenny.

"You're talking back again, Kenny," she said. "And you don't know what you're saying. You disturbed the dust of the others, Kenny! You made them restless and hungry!"

"You're nuts!" said Kenny. "Let me out of here."

"You'll *earn* your way out, like the others!" Miss Payne snapped, her eyes wide and glaring now. "They disobeyed me, too! They've been in a longer detention than you, Kenny, but you are about to join them! You will make up for my mistake yesterday. You will replace Candace Golding—she was the sweet smell in the dust when you first came in. I didn't mean for that to happen. She just came back for a book at the wrong time. I must release her."

"Miss Payne," said Kenny, his voice beginning to quiver now, "I don't understand what you are saying!"

Miss Payne reached over and opened her briefcase. A black shadow swirled up and hovered over Miss Payne's head.

"The spirits of the bad kids," she laughed madly. "You might call them my erasers! They live in the chalkboard as one. They help me get rid of my problems, Kenny, and I help them.

Scared in School

Right now, they are hungry, so I'll feed them. You'll have to be changed to another form, of course! Maybe someday I'll release all of you if you're very, very good!"

She threw back her head and laughed again. The black shadow over her shoulder began to swirl. Faster and faster it turned, and then it headed toward Kenny.

Kenny ran for the door. For one small second, he grasped the hope that he might make it. But it was too late. The shadow swirled around him and swept him up. He saw the desks below before he merged with the shadow. Then he felt the cold, hard surface of the chalkboard and nothing more. The dust of Kenny Phillips settled down on the chalk tray and the erasers.

Slay Ground

Mr. Yates and Miss Payne smiled as the last students boarded the buses. It was their last day of bus duty for the year and their thoughts were on all that had happened at the three schools on 13th Street since last fall.

"I think I'll sponsor more extracurricular activities next year," said Miss Payne. "I have some new things I want to try out. I'm looking forward to a new student body."

"Good idea," agreed Mr. Yates. "It's always good to try new things with new students. New blood and all."

Late afternoon fog drifted in patches from the river and curled around the counselor and teacher. Then it rose like ghosts and vanished. Mr. Yates and Miss Payne laughed and walked by the playground sign to the faculty parking lot.

Kirk Radborne watched the fog from the sidewalk on his way home. He waved to Mr. Yates, who raised his hand. Kirk saw that he was holding a shiny object that looked familiar. Mr. Yates pointed the object at Kirk, and a sharp pain jolted Kirk's head. It lasted only a second. Then Kirk bounded down the street. He felt programmed and energized.

The custodian watching from the hall window saw the sign change from PLAYGROUND to SLAY GROUND and back again, but he would keep that secret so the children would come next year to play.

Low thunder announced the coming of summer, but the flash that briefly lit the sky in the woods behind 13th Street warned that something besides summer's light and warmth was on its way. That something was the ship bringing more of his kind from their dying planet. He would keep that secret, too. To live as earthlings, they had to examine many. His studies this year had been vital. He already had other projects in mind. He thought of all those who would be scared in school next year. Then he swished his mop down the hall. He would be ready as always on opening day.

———————————————